Carry On Doctor

The wickedly funny story that
starts where the film ends

Norman Giller

Chameleon

First published in Great Britain in 1996 by
Chameleon Books
106 Great Russell Street,
London WC1B 3LJ

CIP data for this title is available
from the British Library

ISBN 0 233 99027 5

Typeset by Falcon Oast Graphic Art

Printed in Great Britain by WBC, Bridgend

For Eileenalanna
The light and laugh of my life

Author's Acknowledgements

This book could not have been written without the original foundation work of *Carry On* film creators Peter Rogers and Gerald Thomas. I have simply carried on where they left off, but I would not even have managed the first step without their marathon screen productions to inspire me. I am also indebted to the *Carry On* team of actors, who brought their characters to life on screen and turned the film series into a national institution. I acknowledge, too, the beautifully crafted screenplays of the writers, in particular Talbot Rothwell and Norman Hudis. On behalf of the Publishers, I thank the Rank Organisation for allowing us to step into the *Carry On* territory that has always been exclusive to the silver screen, and for their permission to use still photographs from the original film version of *Carry On Doctor*.

My thanks also to VCI Chief Executive Steve Ayres for letting me off the leash, and to Tim Forrester, Tom Rosenthal and John Cleary at Chameleon Books for their encouragement; also to my House Editor Stephanie Goodwin, and to Richard Percy, who first had the brainwave to turn the *Carry On* films into books. Most of all, thanks to Eileenalanna, Lisa and Michael for being there.

The characters and events depicted on the following pages are entirely fictitious, and anybody who wishes to argue otherwise will be laughed out of court. *Carry On Laughing...*

Introduction

This book carries on where the film *Carry On Doctor**
left off. The story so far:

Dr James Kilmore (Jim Dale) is sacked for misconduct
after being found in a compromising situation with
Nurse May (Barbara Windsor) at the nurse's hostel. Dr
Kilmore is reinstated following a patients' revolt led by
Syd Roper (Sidney James), Charlie Baron (Charles
Hawtrey) and Bernie Biddle (Bernard Bresslaw). They
knew that Kilmore had been set up by the scheming
matron (Hattie Jacques) and the unlikely object of her
sexual desires, Dr Kenneth Tinkle (Kenneth Williams).
Francis Bigger (Frankie Howerd), a bogus faith-
healer, has lost all faith in the health service after
mistakenly being led to believe that he has only forty-
eight hours to live. He reluctantly goes ahead with

*The classic comedy films *Carry On Doctor* and *Carry On Again
Doctor* are both available in the *Carry On* series on Cinema Club
videos, distributed by VCI, price £4.99 each.

something he had been putting off for eleven years – marriage to his long-suffering, hard of hearing fiancée Chloe Gibson (Joan Sims).

The stuttering, stone-deaf hospital chaplain (Peter Jones) conducts a bedside ceremony which takes twice as long as usual because neither the bride nor the chaplain can hear a word that is being said. Rings and vows have just been exchanged when Bigger finds out that the two days he thought he had to live were actually the forty-eight hours in which he was required to get out of hospital to make way for genuinely ill patients. He looks at his wife on their wedding night and considers suing the hospital for saving his life.

Absent-minded surgeon Harmon Hardcastle (Deryck Guyler) has lost a watch while in the operating theatre. It is found ticking away inside a patient who thought he had a nervous tick.

As usual it is complete chaos at Haven Hospital, somewhere on the outskirts of London. Abandon all hope ye who enter here and suspend all belief.

Carry On Reading...

1

D R JAMES KILMORE was testing his new stethoscope on the ample chest of Nurse May. 'Oooh, doctor, your end is cold,' she giggled. 'Let me warm it up for you.'

Before Kilmore could take her up on her thoughtful invitation they were interrupted by the shrill ringing of the telephone. He looked wild-eyed at the bedside clock. 'Who's calling you at two o'clock in the morning?' he asked, a quiver of fear in his voice.

'How do I know until I answer it?' Nurse May said, reaching across him and almost pulling off his ears as the stethoscope got caught in the hook of her right arm.

'For goodness sake don't let anybody know I'm here,' he said in a strangled whisper. 'You know I'm not allowed in the nurses' hostel. It nearly got me the sack last year.'

Nurse May picked up the receiver. 'Hello, who's this?'

She pulled a face as a voice crackled in her ear, and then handed the telephone to Kilmore. 'It's for you,' she said. 'Sounds like a right nutter.'

'For me?' Kilmore spluttered. 'Here? Who knows I'm with you?'

Nurse May shrugged. 'Search me, but he knows you well 'cos he asked for Dr Strangelove.'

Kilmore took the telephone with a mixture of relief and resignation on his face. There was only one person who called him Strangelove, and that was the senior physician at the hospital, Dr Kenneth Tinkle. It was a nickname he'd given him after he had caught him making love to one of the nurses on the operating table. 'It looked to me,' he had said in his peculiar nasal tones, 'as if you were trying to take her tonsils out. But that thing you were using was not like any other scalpel that I've seen.' He had not reported him and they had been close pals and confidants ever since.

'Why are you 'phoning me here, Ken? You know it's out of bounds.'

Kilmore could hardly hear the reply. 'You'll have to speak up, Ken. It's a terrible line.'

He was able to hear perfectly well, however, once the quick-thinking Nurse May reached up and pulled the stethoscope out of his ears.

'We're d-o-o-m-e-d,' came into his ear from Dr Tinkle, who was either very distressed or very drunk. Or possibly both.

'Got to meet you. Now!' Tinkle was shouting in a panic-propelled voice. 'They're out to get us. We've got to stop them. What are we going to do?'

'I can't talk to you here,' said Kilmore, remembering where he was and that he should be whispering. 'We'll wake up the entire hostel. Can't it wait until the morning?'

'It is the morning, and it won't wait.' Tinkle was almost crying into the telephone. 'I'll meet you at the hospital in an hour. The staff room.'

Kilmore suddenly had a telephone line buzzing in his ear. Tinkle had replaced his receiver.

He looked sadly at Nurse May. 'I'm afraid Daddy

Bear has got to go, Goldilocks,' he said. 'I'll have to come and have my oats another day.'

'You can come and take my pulse any time, Doctor,' she said, squeezing him where he wouldn't show his mum. 'You know what they say – underneath every successful man there's a woman.'

She released a cackling laugh that was so loud the doctor pushed a pillow across her mouth. 'Shush,' he said, 'you'll wake Ironknickers and I'll be kicked out of the hospital again.'

Kilmore reluctantly pulled himself out of bed and dressed in the dark, reaching around blindly for the clothes that Nurse May had helped remove from him in a frenzy of passion.

So it was that Dr Kilmore started his slow descent from Nurse May's second-floor window with his Fair Isle sweater and underpants on back to front, with only one sock on and with the nurse's brassiere hooked onto the back of his shirt collar. Clinging precariously to the drainpipe, he had reached the first-floor window below when suddenly the curtains were drawn back and he found himself looking into the sour face of the dreaded hostel supervisor, known behind her back as Miss Ironknickers.

She was not wearing her usual pebble glasses, and neither was she wearing her teeth. Kilmore had seen more appealing sights at Brighton Aquarium. The supervisor squinted through the window at him and he had the presence of mind to pull a handkerchief from his trouser pocket and start wiping each pane of glass.

Miss Ironknickers pulled up the window. It took all

Kilmore's strength not to fall back as he clung on desperately to the drainpipe with one hand while waving his handkerchief like a flag of surrender with the other. 'And just what do you think you're doing?' she demanded.

'Very sorry to disturb you, missus,' he said in gruff Cockney tones. 'We're short-staffed down at the window cleaning office, like, and so I'm having to do a night shift.'

'Well just do it quietly and don't wake any of my gals,' she said, slamming the window closed so quickly that it trapped the fingers of Kilmore's left hand.

He banged at the window with his head until the dreaded Miss Ironknickers reappeared.

She re-opened the window. 'What's that banging?'

'It's the wind, a real howler,' Kilmore said, pulling his bruised fingers free. 'I think I'll pack it in for the night. Sweet dreams, missus.'

The doctor was relieved to see Ironknickers close the curtains, and then continued his climb down the drainpipe. He had just touched terra firma when he was startled out of his wits by somebody tapping on his shoulder.

'Hello, hello, hello... caught you red-handed, ain't I?'

Kilmore turned round to find himself looking up into the smug face of PC Shufflebottom from the local police station. He stood six foot five inches tall without his helmet, and he cast a giant shadow over the doctor.

'Well, well, well, if it ain't the one and only Dr Kildare,' said the constable.

'Kilmore,' said Kilmore.

'Breaking and entering, eh? That's serious, that is. Very serious.'

'I'm exiting, not entering.'

Kilmore and Shufflebottom were old adversaries. During a hospital rag five years earlier he had run off with the police constable's helmet and filled it with horse manure. Shufflebottom had put it on without realising, and had been known at the local nick ever since as Stinker Shufflebottom.

'You'd better have a good reason for climbing down that drainpipe, or you're going to end up in the dock, Doc.' Shufflebottom started to laugh. 'Doc, dock! Geddit? In the dock, Doc.'

Kilmore considered a play on the word constable but thought better of it.

'I was making a house call,' he said.

'In the nurses' hostel?'

'That's right. There was a nurse in urgent need of chest manipulation treatment.'

Shufflebottom was very nearly salivating. 'Which one was it?'

'Uh, the right one.'

'No, I mean which nurse?'

'Nurse May. Second floor.'

'Cor, you lucky what's it. She's the one with the huge knockers, ain't she?'

Kilmore nodded, nearly blinded by the gleam in the constable's eye.

'We're mad on her down at the station, we are. We even beat up prisoners so that we can take them down to casualty and have a gander at her.'

'I admire your taste,' said Kilmore, desperately trying to think of a way out of Shufflebottom's clutches. It would cost him his career if he were again reported for having a night of nookie in the nurses' hostel. The last time it was only a revolt by the hospital patients that saved his skin.

It was Shufflebottom who came up with the solution.

'Tell you what, Doc,' he said conspiratorially, 'I'll forget I saw you climbing down the drainpipe if you can fix me up with a date with Nurse May. We've got a bet on down at the station, and the first one lucky enough to take her out wins the pot.'

'No trouble at all, old chap,' said Kilmore. 'I'll have a word with her when she's next on duty and tell her that a good friend of mine wants to take her out to show her a good time.'

'That's not all I'll show her, eh Doc!' Shufflebottom said, nudging the wind out of Kilmore with an elbow in the ribs. 'You're a clever Dick, Doc.'

Shufflebottom started laughing again, this time uncontrollably. 'Geddit? A clever Dick, Doc.'

He was now laughing so loudly that he was waking the nurses. The light went back on in the room of Miss Ironknickers and her window was noisily pulled open.

'Go away you dirty stop-outs,' she shouted, 'or I'll call the police.'

That finished Shufflebottom off. He fell to the floor with tears rolling down his cheeks. Kilmore waved goodbye and hurried to his drop bars racing bike parked by the railings opposite the hostel. He mounted the bike and had gone half a circulation of the front wheel when he was rudely reminded that it is advisable to first unchain the bike from the fence.

Dr Kilmore briefly continued his journey *sans* bike, sailing over the handlebars and landing nose first on the pavement. He picked himself up and staunched the flow of blood from a gash on the bridge of his nose with the same handkerchief with which he had cleaned the hostel supervisor's windows. Mixed in with the blood on his face he now had a smear of grease, and he looked like a Red Indian preparing for war. Kilmore reached into the first-aid bag on the rear of his bicycle and slapped a large piece of white sticking plaster onto his nose.

He then unchained the bike and rode off into the night with the constable still on his knees laughing like a mad man. 'A date with Nurse May?' he said aloud to himself as he pedalled furiously towards the hospital. 'Stinker Shufflebottom should not hold his breath.'

Upstairs, Miss Ironknickers was making a 999 call to report that a maniac was loose outside the nurse's hostel. 'Don't worry,' said the station sergeant, 'our very own PC Shufflebottom is on his beat and will be arriving in that area any moment now.'

'Everything all right, sir?' asked Clarence, the night-duty porter, as Kilmore arrived breathlessly at the hospital entrance.

'Fine, thank you, Clarence. Has Dr Tinkle arrived by any chance?'

'Yes, sir. About twenty minutes ago. Didn't seem his usual cheerful self. Is there something up, sir? Something I can help with?'

15

'Not that I know of, but the way you're staring at me, Clarence, makes me wonder if you think there's something wrong with me.'

'Staring, sir? Not me, sir.'

Clarence had been a porter at Haven Hospital for more than twenty years and had grown accustomed to the peculiarities of the staff, particularly the doctors. 'No problems, sir,' he said. 'I quite understand if Sir wants to wear a bra hanging down his back. Who am I to question the genius of a doctor?'

Kilmore swivelled his neck and caught sight of the bra dangling from his collar. He reached behind him and pulled it free, stuffing it inside his back-to-front pullover.

'I'm, uh, just looking after it for a friend,' he spluttered. 'I wanted to keep it in a conspicuous place so that I'd know where to find it. It'd look odd if I wore it on my chest, wouldn't it?'

'Yes, fairly odd, sir, but there's no need for explanations. You do whatever you want. The hours you have to work you're entitled to a little eccentricity. What you want, sir, is a good strong union behind you. They treat you doctors and nurses as if this is the 1860s rather than the 1960s. It's a bloody disgrace, pardon my French.'

Kilmore spread his arms in a 'so-what-can-I-do-about-it?' gesture. 'I'm busting for a pee, Clarence. All right if I use the porter's toilet?'

A pained expression stretched across Clarence's lugubrious face. 'Sorry, sir, but it's against our union rules. Doctors and nurses must use their own toilet facilities. More than my job's worth to let you use the porter loo, sir.'

'Not to worry,' said Kilmore. 'I'll use the one in casualty.'

'No can do, sir. Sorry. It's closed while the night cleaners are in.'

'So where's the nearest loo that I *can* use?'

'For you, sir, that'll be the second floor, next to your staff room. Incidentally, that is where Dr Tinkle said he would see you.'

Tinkle. Not the word that Kilmore wanted to hear just at that moment. He dashed to the lift and pushed the button. It was three minutes before it made a clanking arrival, by which time he was hopping from foot to foot with a boiler that was ready to burst. He was concentrating too hard on matters in hand to realise that the lift was going down rather than up. When he got out at what he thought was the second floor he was actually in the basement.

Kilmore raced blindly along the corridor to where the staff room toilet would have been were he on the correct floor. When he arrived at his destination he almost went purple as he found he was staring at a door that read MORTUARY.

He was now at the point of no return. He pushed open the mortuary door and rushed in, looking desperately for any place where he could relieve himself of his growing burden. The night mortuary attendant almost fainted when the perspiring Kilmore charged in, with the bra dangling down from below his back-to-front pullover and the white plaster on his nose now soaked a bloody crimson.

'What the fu..?' the startled mortuary assistant began to say.

'Sorry, old chap,' said Kilmore. 'Got to pee or I'll explode.'

Lying on the slab was a naked body waiting for a post-mortem. In its hands, locked in the rigor mortis of the dead man's grip, was a flower vase he had been holding when he died. Kilmore unzipped his trousers and reached for his now throbbing member.

He fumbled around and then stumbled against the slab.

'God help me!' he cried. 'I've lost my John Thomas.'

The mortuary attendant was flat against the wall, looking around wildly to see what he could lay his hands on with which to defend himself against this maniac.

Now it dawned on Kilmore that he had got his underpants on back to front, and as he started to take off his trousers the mortuary attendant ran out, shouting, 'Oh no you don't. You're not going to have me, mate. And you leave that poor corpse alone, you bloody necrophiliac you.'

Kilmore was oblivious to the effect his crazed entrance had had on the mortuary attendant. All he was interested in was having his pee. At last he had his best friend in his hand and, with small pearls of perspiration bubbling on his brow, started to fill the vase in the dead man's hands.

It was at this point that the mortuary attendant arrived back with Clarence in tow. They stood watching open-mouthed from the doorway as Kilmore sent a yellow stream arrowing into the vase.

'Don't worry,' Clarence said to the mortuary attendant. 'That's Dr Kilmore. He's *allowed* to be eccentric.'

2

Kᴇɴɴᴇᴛʜ ᴛɪɴᴋʟᴇ was in a state of almost frothing agitation when Kilmore finally arrived at the staff room.

'At last, at last, somebody I can talk to,' he said, virtually pulling Kilmore through the door. 'I'm carrying a secret that is weighing me down like a bag of dung. I'm absolutely desperate to share it with you.'

'Calm down, Ken,' Kilmore said, adopting the unlikely role of father confessor. 'Take a deep breath and then tell me everything. I'll be your rock. Come on now. Open up and let it all out.'

Tinkle was just about to unburden himself when he did a double take as he took his first proper look at Kilmore. 'What on earth are you doing with a bra hanging from your jersey?... why have you got your jersey on back to front?... what's that bloody plaster on your nose?... and what are you doing with that flower vase in your hands?'

Kilmore pulled the bra out and tucked it under a cushion on the sofa. He placed the vase on the mantelpiece, and then tugged off his pullover and put it back on the right way round.

'Just tell me about the vase for now,' pleaded Tinkle. 'It's breaking my concentration.'

'It belongs to a chap lying in the mortuary,' Kilmore explained in a matter-of-fact way. 'Clarence said that because I'd peed in it the union rules were that none of his staff were allowed to empty it, so I've brought it up here and will empty it later.'

'Uh, yes, I think I see,' said Tinkle. 'Now listen to this...'

He looked around the empty room to make sure nobody was eavesdropping. Then he opened the door, furtively glanced out into the corridor and came back in, satisfied that he had the ears only of Kilmore. He stood close and spoke in a hoarse whisper.

'They're going to knock down the hospital and build a supermarket,' he said dramatically.

'They're going to do what?' said Kilmore, none of it sinking in or making sense at the first time of telling.

'They're going to knock down the hospital and build a supermarket,' Tinkle repeated, his eyes bulging and his nostrils almost flaring with the strain and excitement of it all.

'How do you know?'

'Matilda.'

'Matilda?'

'The Mayor's secretary.'

'That tall, slim brunette you've been rogering for weeks? The one that hides her best points under layers of clothing?'

'That's the one. At the height of our how's your father last night she suddenly started to sob. God, I thought, I've really made the earth move for her. But then she started saying, "Poor Kenneth. What's going to become of you?"'

'And then?'

'Well, after making me promise on my mother's life

– the old dear passed on years ago – that I wouldn't tell a soul, she confided that the Mayor and half a dozen leading councillors have done a deal with a property developer. They're going to have Haven Hospital declared an unsafe building, raze it to the ground and have one of those new-fangled supermarkets built in its place.'

'They can't do that.'

'Who's going to stop them?'

'The government. Harold Wilson wouldn't allow it.'

'That's what I said, but Matilda assures me that Labour arms will be twisted and manipulated to make sure there's no interference.'

Kilmore slumped down on the sofa, his mind in turmoil. As he crossed his legs, Tinkle tried to ignore the fact that he was wearing only one sock.

'This is an enormous calamity,' said Kilmore. 'Where will the local people be without Haven? Almost as worrying, where will *we* be? There's not another hospital who would ever employ us, not with our disciplinary records.'

'I know, I know,' whined Tinkle. 'Reports of your peccadillos could fill a wall, and I've been blacklisted ever since I spurned Matron's amorous advances.'

He shuddered and closed his eyes. 'God, it was like having a rhinoceros coming at me,' he recalled. 'I tried hard to lie back and think of England, but she ruptured my epiglottis and I passed out. She gave me the kiss of life and when I came round I saw her hovering over me and screamed. Clarence came bursting into the room, and the sight of Matron's colossal bare bum staring at

22

him had a profound effect. Clarence and Matron have been inseparable ever since, and she's gone and turned all vindictive and spiteful against me.'

While listening to Tinkle's nightmare reminiscence, Kilmore unconsciously picked the bra up from beneath the cushion and was twisting it nervously in his hands.

'That's a minor problem,' he said. 'There will be no Matron, no Clarence, no doctors, no gorgeous nurses and no patients if Haven is closed down. We've *got* to stop them.'

He stood up and gave Tinkle a reassuring hug. 'We're not going to let the bastards beat us,' he promised. 'We'll have the Mayor by his balls.'

They were still hugging as the door swung open and a night-duty nurse came in. 'Oops, sorry to interrupt,' she said, blushing crimson. 'I was looking for something.'

The two doctors pulled away from each other as if they'd had a sudden electric shock. 'It's not what you think,' said Tinkle. 'We're just good friends.'

Kilmore held out the bra. 'Is this, uh, what you're looking for? I just found it on the sofa.'

The nurse blushed a deeper red. 'No, this is what I came for.' She went to the mantelpiece and took the vase containing Kilmore's urine. 'We mislaid this specimen.'

She collected the vase and went back out of the door, with Kilmore making silent goldfish movements with his mouth.

'What are we going to do?' said Tinkle, now in a state of panic. 'What's going to become of us? Without my job I would be finished, washed-up, a useless wreck...'

'Pull yourself together, man,' Kilmore shouted.

'But I'm done for... I'm a broken man... you're a doctor, you know this is all I've ever wanted... you understand what this means to me... it's my vocation... it's my whole life... it's my *raison d'être*...'

At this point Clarence came in, just as Kilmore slapped Tinkle around the face to try to snap him out of his hysteria.

Clarence did not bat an eyelid. 'Just to let you know, sirs, that there has been a serious road smash involving a coach. All doctors are to report to casualty.'

Tinkle, with duty calling, calmed down immediately. Kilmore lightly punched him on the shoulder. 'Come on, Ken. All hands on deck, Doc. On deck, Doc? Get it? Am I a clever Dick, Doc? Or should I be in the dock, Doc? Stinker Shufflebottom thought it was funny.'

Tinkle could not take it in. 'What are you babbling on about? And what happened to your nose?'

'Uh, I forgot to duck, Doc.'

They walked together into the corridor, Kilmore still holding the bra.

'Let's get this emergency out of the way,' he said, 'and then I shall outline a plan that is beginning to develop in my mind. The Mayor is going to have his chain pulled.'

Tinkle decided to have the last word. 'I still don't know,' he said, 'why you've only got one sock, Doc.'

There were four hours of bloody bedlam in casualty before Drs Kilmore and Tinkle returned to the staff

24

room in a state of utter exhaustion, neither of them having slept since the previous night. Tinkle poured himself a black coffee and then dropped heavily onto the sofa alongside Kilmore.

'So what's the great plan?' he asked. 'How are we going to stop the wicked Mayor wrecking my life?'

Kilmore's reply was a deep snore. He had fallen asleep the moment he sank into the sofa.

'That's bloody marvellous, that is,' Tinkle said aloud to himself. 'Here am I faced with the crisis of a lifetime and he just lies there snoring. What am I going to do?'

'Well, you can lift your feet for a start, luv. I've got to vacuum here,' said Mrs Wilton, the hospital cleaner.

Tinkle sat bolt upright, spilling his steaming-hot coffee into the lap of Kilmore who awoke with a scream. The scalding liquid had landed just as he slipped into a dream in which he was lying on a mortuary slab with PC Shufflebottom about to pee all over him. 'Into the vase, not on me you imbecile,' he shouted.

Mrs Wilton looked on unmoved. She was from the Clarence school of hospital workers who accepted that all doctors were a little on the mad side.

'I didn't know you were in here, Mrs Wilton,' said Tinkle. 'Frightened the living daylights out of me.'

'This is my staff room cleaning time,' she explained. 'I'll have to shoo you doctors out. Can't have you interfering with my work schedule. Clarence, our union organiser, would do his marbles.'

Kilmore, still half asleep, got to his feet and walked zombie-like towards the door. His feet became entangled in the vacuum lead and he fell headlong to the floor, crashing his head against the skirting board.

He reeled around like a battered boxer as Tinkle helped him to his feet, finally bringing him under control by hanging on to his braces.

'Oh, by the way, Doctor,' Mrs Wilton called as Tinkle pulled the door open ready to lead the confused Kilmore to the sanctuary of the sleeping quarters on the next floor.

Tinkle looked back over his shoulder. 'Yes, Mrs Wilton?'

'That problem of yours,' she said. 'A good slap will sort the wicked mare out, take it from me. My old man swears by it.'

Kilmore had been concussed by his fall, and Tinkle kept hold of him by his braces as they walked unsteadily down the corridor towards the lift. The night nurse who had seen them together in an embrace earlier that morning was just coming off duty, and was standing at the lift when they arrived like a pair of drunks.

They followed the nurse into the lift, and she pressed herself into a corner as far away from them as she could manage. Tinkle felt he owed her an explanation.

'What you saw earlier,' he said, 'when you caught the pair of us hugging... it was not what it seemed, I promise you.'

The nurse, trying hard not to look at the dark, steaming stain around the groin area of Kilmore's trousers, shrugged. 'It doesn't matter,' she said. 'I quite understand. I have several gay friends.'

26

'You've got the wrong end of the stick, my dear,' Tinkle insisted. 'We were just feeling emotional about some news we'd been given. I assure you that there's nothing *that way* about either of us.'

Kilmore, with Tinkle still keeping him upright by his braces, was swaying back and forth wearing a silly grin on his face and a glazed look in his eyes. The ancient lift shuddered as it stopped at the third floor, and Kilmore's braces snapped as he fell away from Tinkle's grasp and his trousers slipped down to his knees. He bumped his head against the door, and as it slid open he tumbled face first out into the corridor right at the feet of the Matron, who was just about to start her early morning perambulations.

'What is the meaning of this?' she demanded. 'How dare you come into the hospital in this condition.'

'He's not inebriated, Matron,' Tinkle explained. 'He's just had a bang in the lift.'

Matron looked daggers at the nurse who was on her knees alongside Kilmore, studying an egg-size bruise on the doctor's forehead.

'Leave him be, nurse,' she ordered. 'Get on with your duties to the patients. They *really* need your help.'

'But I've just come off duty,' the nurse said.

'Don't answer back. Do as you're told. This instant. You know the hospital rules about nurses not mixing socially with the doctors.'

'We've not been mixing,' Tinkle protested. 'We just met in the lift.'

'Yes,' said Matron, 'and I'm Queen of the May.'

'It's going to need a gigantic Maypole,' Tinkle

muttered as an aside.

Matron's face was set in concrete. 'I heard that, Dr Tinkle,' she snapped. 'Don't be so facetious. As senior physician of this hospital you should be setting a better example. '

She pointed down at the slumped figure of Kilmore. 'Now get this drunken toad back to his quarters and let him sleep it off. I will be making a full report on this incident to the board of governors.'

Tinkle gave a two-fingered salute in the direction of her departing back as she disappeared into the lift, which quite startled the hospital chaplain who was passing her on his way out of the lift. He responded with a sign of the cross.

'B-b-b-bless you, my son,' the chaplain shouted in the belief that everybody was as deaf as himself. He looked at the prostrate figure of Kilmore, and then crouched down to get a closer look.

'My goodness, it's our Dr K-K-K-Kilmore,' he stuttered. 'Would you b-b-b-believe it. Whatever's happened to the poor man?'

'He's bumped his head,' said Tinkle.

'Fell out of b-b-b-bed?' said the chaplain. 'That was rather careless of him. I'll say a prayer for him in the hospital ch-ch-ch-chapel.'

'You can say one for me while you're about it,' said Tinkle.

'One what?' bellowed the chaplain.

'A prayer,' shouted Tinkle.

'A p-p-pair of what?'

'Oh, forget it.'

'Get what?'

'God help us.'

'Yes, my son. G-G-G-God help us all. I shall also say a p-p-p-prayer for you.'

The chaplain gave the sign of the cross again before stepping over the flattened Kilmore and continuing on his way to the chapel. Tinkle quietly cursed under his breath as he hauled Kilmore up and half dragged and half carried him to the staff sleeping quarters.

He dropped Kilmore backwards onto his bed as if delivering a sack of coal.

'When you come back to your senses I hope you can remember your master plan,' he said. 'Otherwise we'll have to try following Mrs Wilton's advice and give the Mayor a slap.'

Kilmore responded with a grin. He was already fast asleep and dreaming of Nurse May and her greatest assets. Goldilocks and Daddy Bear would have all their oats.

3

WHILE DR KILMORE was sleeping the day away, Mayor William Cocklewell was sitting in his Town Hall office preparing to push ahead with his top-secret plan to replace the hospital with a supermarket. He summoned his secretary, Matilda Thrush. 'It's time for Dick Tation, Tilly,' he said slowly and deliberately, patting his ample thighs to indicate that he wanted her to join him behind rather than at his desk. 'I want you to take something down, ho, ho, ho!'

As usual, Matilda coldly ignored his clumsy sexual innuendo. She warded off at least a dozen advances a week. Her revenge for the latest approach would come quietly in the form of afternoon tea lightly laced with bromide. 'The day will dawn,' she silently comforted herself, 'when I will lead the fight to stamp out this sort of obnoxious sexual harassment.'

Matilda, a closet man-hater except when it suited her needs, had worked with the Council since leaving the local grammar school nine years earlier with seven 'O' levels and a desire to get into politics. She had wanted to go to university, but needed to leave school at sixteen to help supplement her mother's meagre wages after her father had walked out for a younger woman. Her mother had since worked at poisoning her mind against all men, something she found came naturally without need of constant coaxing.

Matilda had classic features and a heavenly body that

she kept hidden away under shapeless sweaters and ankle-length skirts. The few men she had allowed to plumb her depths were surprised and delighted to find beneath the layers of clothes a figure that would have done credit to a Hollywood screen goddess, but she deliberately hid it away from the gaze of male chauvinists like William Cocklewell.

She sat opposite the Mayor, shorthand pencil poised above her notebook and wishing that it was a knife that she could jab into his enormous stomach that lay in folds over his brown leather belt. As an unnecessary insurance, he also wore wide red braces round which he hooked his thumbs while dictating as he paced the office. He was Mr Vanity, convinced that nobody knew that he was virtually bald. A ginger wig perched on his head like a dormant hamster was the subject of much merriment behind his back.

His letters were collectors' items of grammatical gobbledegook which Matilda did nothing to correct. She secretly despised her boss with a passion that could be measured on the Richter scale, and was only staying in her job because she had a plan of her own to stop what she saw as his disgraceful and criminal fortune-making supermarket scheme.

Matilda had already, quite literally, made contact with a doctor at the hospital, who she was sure would be able to help her torpedo the Mayor. When she had outlined the supermarket plan to him in bed on their last date Matilda had been overwhelmed by his reaction. Dr Tinkle had started to cry. She then realised that he was not only highly sexed but also highly strung.

The Mayor had lit up a giant Churchillian cigar, and his strident tones were a sudden and unwelcome intrusion on her train of thought.

'Reet, this is for the confidential attention of 'aven 'ospital secretary Mr C A Clutterbuck,' the Mayor said with his Yorkshire accent as distinctive as the day he left Bradford thirty-seven years before in search of gold on London's pavements. All he had found was dirt and grime, but he had used a Midas touch to turn this into gold by following the old Yorkshire dictum of 'where there's muck, there's brass.' He had set up an office-cleaning business, first of all providing an army of chars to clean inside and then a scaffolding company for outside repairs and refurbishment in the immediate postwar years when London buildings were blackened with soot and smoke.

The 'Clean Air Act' of 1956 was, to his mind, a treacherous piece of legislation that might have improved the health of the hoi polloi but which seriously damaged his wealth. He had turned to the property world to compensate for a fall-off in the office-restoration business, and as chairman of the housing committee had a fat hand in several lucrative development contracts. Now, with just three months left of his year in office as Mayor, he was on the brink of his greatest coup. Harry Hopper, self-styled supermarket king, had promised him his own life-long cash till if he could guarantee him being able to open a new American-style supermarket on the three acres of land occupied by the hospital.

The Mayor started to pace the office as he searched for the right words to lay the foundation for what would be the ultimate closure of the hospital. He drew hard on his cigar, convinced it gave him the sort of word power for which his idol Winston Churchill was famous. He was proud to share the great man's initials, although there were those who sniggered that W C was appropriate for another reason. With a sudden rush of inspiration, he started to dictate.

'Dear Mr Clutterbuck,' he began, "aven 'ospital 'as become a bloody death trap and a reet shyte ole. I 'ave 'ere on my desk 'undreds, aye, 'undreds of letters of complaint about the state of t'building.'

He broke off for an aside. 'Make a note, Tilly, that we must get some complaint letters written.'

The Mayor then returned to his dictation of a letter that made Matilda's skin crawl with every sentence. 'Falling masonry is a threat to the precious lives of the citizens of this borough, and inside the 'ospital there are reported to be leaking pipes, rotting wood, bug-infested beds, dangerously loose floorboards that could give thee a nasty blow to the cobblers if they were to suddenly spring up like, and the state of the pigsty kitchens are so bad that the cockroaches are said to search for indigestion tablets...'

He exploded with laughter that gave ground to a cough as he inhaled too much cigar smoke. 'D'you like that one, Tilly? Cockroaches searching for indigestion tablets. I don't know where I get them from. I really don't. Should 'ave been a comedian.'

Matilda resisted the urge to tell him that he was the biggest joke she knew and sat waiting for the next dictated pearl.

'As chairman of the 'ousing, 'ospital and works committee for this borough, make that this blessed borough, it is my responsibility to see to it that everything is kept in good order, nay excellent order. Pursuant to this... I like that, pursuant to this... I am sending an 'ealth and safety inspector to make a full report on 'aven 'ospital, and if his findings are what I expect I will 'ave no alternative but to recommend the closure of said 'ospital because it's making people iller instead of better.'

The Mayor smiled to himself. His health and safety officer was his old drinking pal Percy Dick, who would put anything into his report for fifty smackers in the hand. He had once helped the Mayor get the old Ritz cinema in the town centre closed down by reporting that it had enough fleas in it to start a circus. What was not in the report is that Percy himself had planted sufficient fleas to fill a dog's home before making his inspection. Mayor Cocklewell was sure that for a couple of hundred smackers he would make Haven Hospital sound like the black hole of Calcutta.

The hospital was already in a genuinely run down condition, but that was chiefly because in his role as adviser to the borough council treasury department he had ensured that improvement funds were never available. He assuaged his conscience by convincing himself that the mushrooming world of private hospitals was the way forward.

He suddenly spoke his private thoughts aloud and Matilda shorthanded them down into the letter. 'The National 'ealth is done for. It's not 'ospital beds this

34

borough needs, but shopping baskets... wire ones on wheels that you push around like a pram. That's the future. It will bring prosperity and prosperity will bring good 'ealth. The bloody National 'ealth is an unnecessary drain on this country's economy.'

The Mayor pulled on his cigar, not realising that Matilda had noted his last comments. As reading had never been one of his specialist subjects, he did not bother to try to read the letters he dictated. All he did was sign them. He knew he could trust Matilda, who he had inherited as his secretary from the previous Mayor who claimed she was totally trustworthy and scrupulously honest – virtues that had marked his predecessor's year of office but which had never been allowed to cramp the style of the present incumbent. The Mayor was disappointed that Matilda had not yet allowed him any sexual favours, but he was sure that was only a matter of time provided he kept up his charm offensive. He felt pretty sure that under those appallingly sexless clothes was a real woman waiting to get out. All he wanted was the slightest encouragement and he would make her body sing to his caresses. What was it Mrs Cocklewell had once said to him in the back of his van nine months before they got married, him with a shotgun nudged in his ribs? 'Oh, Willie,' he remembered her moaning, 'you're like a pit pony on 'eat.' Yes, he was a sex pistol.

'Reet,' said Mayor Cocklewell, 'now to wind up this letter. Add that the council 'ealth and safety inspector, Mr P Dick, will be making an unannounced inspection of the 'ospital in the near future. I will then study his report before deciding what action to take, but be warned that the situation is gravely serious. You could say, Mr Clutterbuck, that the 'aven 'ospital is in intensive care. D'you like that, Tilly? Gives it a bit of colour, don't you think? Now I'll just give it a Churchillian flourish to finish with, and then you can type it out. The final paragraph should read, "This is not the beginning of the end of the 'aven, but it could be the end of the beginning. Your blood, sweat and tears is not enough. What we want is a good, clean and safe 'ospital, otherwise I'll 'ave your guts for garters. My very best wishes, etcetera etcetera..."'

He took a long puff of his cigar. 'Okay, Tilly, that's it. Just two copies, marked very private and very confidential. One copy for me and one for Clutterbuck.'

Mayor Cocklewell snapped his braces back against his chest in a gesture of satisfaction. As Matilda walked past him towards her outer office he lightly patted her on the buttocks.

Matilda clenched her buttocks and her teeth. Then she went to her Remington Noiseless and typed out three copies of the letter.

The original of the letter was hand delivered to Mr Clutterbuck that afternoon, which was an unfortunate bit of timing because it coincided with his daily secret tipple of a bottle of whisky. He had been a member of Alcoholics Anonymous, but changed his name so that he could carry on drinking. The words of the letter were a blur, and added to this was his problem of severe dyslexia. As far as he could make out there had been an outbreak of woodworm caused by leaking pipes, and the Mayor was sending a Mr Dick P for an inspection to see if he could be cured of indigestion brought on by eating cockroaches. Mr Clutterbuck screwed the letter up and tossed it into his wastepaper basket. Dick P would have to take his place in the National Health queue like every other patient.

Matilda personally handed a smuggled copy of the letter to Dr Tinkle, who first of all went to see Clutterbuck for his reaction.

The hospital secretary had his head down on his desk when Tinkle knocked on his door and entered. As Tinkle feared, the letter had arrived just after his daily intake of whisky. To get any sense out of Cuthbert Clutterbuck you needed to get to him before lunch. Sober, he was the best man in the country at his job. Drunk, he was useless to mankind and had a disconcerting habit of wanting to fight the world. The only reason he was kept on at the hospital was that during his sober hours he achieved wonders, doing the work of two men and juggling the finances so that the hospital was just about able to run at the break-even budget demanded by the Council.

Sensing he had company, Clutterbuck pulled himself upright in his chair and made out through the alcoholic haze the foggy outline of Dr Tinkle.

'Ah, tinkle, tinkle little sshstar... how I wonder who you are? If it's not Doctor Tinkle. What can I do you for, old boy?'

'I just wondered, Cuthbert, if you had received a letter from the Mayor?' Tinkle asked, knowing before he had opened his mouth that he was wasting his time.

Clutterbuck started to sing. 'The old town mayor he ain't what he usshhed to be, ain't what he usshhed to be, ain't what he usshhed to be. The old town mayor...'

'Yes, all right,' said Tinkle. 'I'll come back when you're more coherent.'

Coherent, cohabiting. Words that easily sound the same to drunken ears. Clutterbuck was having a clandestine affair with the hospital almoner, and Tinkle had to his muddled mind just made a serious allegation.

'I'm not cohabiting with anybody,' Clutterbuck snapped, dropping into the totally unreasonable and nasty mood that often accompanied his drunkenness. 'And I'll punch you on the noshe if you cahst such aspershions on my character again.'

He came charging from behind his desk and pinned the suddenly petrified Tinkle up against the door. 'Who d'you think you are, eh?' he snarled. 'Jusht 'cosh you've got a doctor'sh degree doeshn't make you any better than me. How dare you shuggesht I'm cohabiting with the almoner. I've a good mind to smash your facshe in.'

Tinkle had an even better mind to get out of the office as swiftly as possible. Clutterbuck had a sudden mood change and released him, then dropped on his knees begging forgiveness. Tinkle spotted the screwed up Mayor's letter in the waste-paper basket and decided to retreat, leaving the now weeping Clutterbuck alone with his drink-induced demons.

He then took his copy of the letter to the still-sleeping Dr Kilmore, and shook him awake.

Kilmore's head was spinning as he sat up. 'Where's

Nurse May?' he asked, looking around through half-closed eyes.

The excited Tinkle shook him by the shoulders. 'I've got it,' he said. 'I've got it.'

'Penicillin tablets will do the trick,' said Kilmore, still not quite sure who or where he was.

'Listen, you knucklehead. I've got the letter.'

'French?'

'The letter about the closure of the hospital.'

They were the words that brought Dr Kilmore back into the real world. 'God, so I've not been dreaming,' he said. 'There really is a plan to close down the hospital.'

Tinkle handed him the letter. 'Read this, and then you'll realise that my information from Matilda was one hundred per cent correct.'

Kilmore, a triangle of blood-crusted white plaster still covering the bridge of his nose, swung his legs out of bed and sat and read the classic prose from Mayor Cocklewell.

'Right,' he said, 'this is war. First of all we've got to get to Clutterbuck to see what action he is planning.'

'I've already been to see him,' said Tinkle. 'He was drowning in his usual sea of whisky. His letter was screwed up in the waste-paper basket. To be frank, nothing has sunk in with him apart from another bottle of scotch.'

'Okay, so it's up to us to save the hospital,' said a suddenly alive and alert Kilmore. 'Bring me my clothes, Kenneth, and it had better be army dress. We're going into battle.'

4

Dr Kilmore addressed the hastily convened meeting in a room above the Crown and Anchor with all the intensity of a general putting his troops on a war footing. He managed to keep his dignity despite the fact that the bottom half of his right trouser leg was missing following an altercation with a Dobermann charged with the job of keeping unwanted visitors away from the private, residential part of the pub. He had wandered into this no-go area because of a simple navigational error when told the meeting room was upstairs on the left. Right, left. It was easy to get the two muddled, particularly when you had your mind full of battle plans.

The landlord had been reasonably understanding after racing upstairs to prise off the Dobermann, and he had informed the ruffled and rueful doctor that the little matter of fifty quid would pay for the furniture damaged when Kilmore and the dog had wrestled their way across the lounge floor. He was kind enough to accept a cheque that just about cleaned out Kilmore's current account.

This venue for the meeting had been selected by Sydney Roper, the former Haven Hospital patient who led the revolt when Kilmore had been threatened with the sack. The doctor had given Roper a rough outline of the closure crisis facing the hospital, and at Kilmore's suggestion he had immediately agreed to organise a gathering of the former Haven Hospital patients who had battled to save Kilmore's job.

From his position on a small stage in the corner of the smoke-filled room usually reserved for union and lodge meetings and small weddings, Kilmore looked proudly down at the men who were once again prepared to stand up and fight for the hospital's rights and for its very existence. Roper, a flattened-nosed ex-professional middleweight boxer, sat with his arms crossed in the second row of wooden chairs. He had sworn undying allegiance to Kilmore ever since the doctor had cured his painful ingrowing toenail, and he considered him a medical genius. A carpenter by trade, he had recently opened his own betting shop in the local high street and was always inviting Kilmore in for a flutter, but the delights of the betting world were lost on the doctor who thought that an each-way Yankee was a bi-sexual American.

Slouched alongside Roper with a look of agony on his face was the weedy figure of the bespectacled Charlie Baron, a library assistant who was once again suffering from his wife's pregnancy symptoms. There were those who thought him somewhat effeminate, and he looked as if a strong wind would blow him over, but when the crunch came he had proved that appearances could be deceptive. In a free-for-all with hospital security guards during the patients' revolt he had sent two of them to casualty with well-aimed kicks to the privates. He had afterwards collapsed with labour pains, and his wife gave birth to twins two hours later. Charlie was now convinced that triplets were on the way.

41

To the left of Baron was Bernie Biddle, a slow-thinking but quick-acting colossus of a man who had recently landed a job with a firm of undertakers. 'What future is there in that?' his girlfriend had said when he told her the news of his appointment. 'That's a dying trade.' Biddle had just been promoted to driving the hearse, and while waiting for Kilmore to start his address had been studying an A-to-Z street guide to try to find out exactly where the cemetery was situated.

Market stallholders Peter 'Granny' Smith and Fred 'Juicy' Apple sat together in the third row alongside self-styled 'The Right Reverend' Francis Bigger. He had been conning a living as a faith-healer until a stay in the Haven when, thinking he was about to meet his maker, he allowed himself to be beguiled into a marriage ceremony with his long-suffering fiancée. He had lost all faith when he found that news of his imminent departure was greatly exaggerated and that he was perfectly healthy. He had even considered suing the hospital for saving his life. 'Ruining it more like,' he had said when looking at his now wife, who could have earned a living haunting houses.

After leaving hospital Bigger, a reluctantly recovering alcoholic, had relaunched himself as an evangelist, armed with a framed certificate of ordination he had bought by mail-order from the American 'Holier Than Thou' church of worship. For appearances sake he always carried a Bible, which was actually hollow and contained a small flask of the finest malt whisky. It gave hidden meaning to his revelation that 'inside here is the answer to all of mankind's problems. And womankind's, missus.'

Dr Tinkle sat on the stage alongside Dr Kilmore, who told his audience in detail of the plan to knock down the hospital to make way for a supermarket. He read them the all-revealing letter to prove the Mayor's intent. When it came to the bit about private hospitals, Charlie Baron shouted, 'Shame on him. Surely he doesn't expect me to pay for the delivery of my next baby?'

Kilmore folded the letter and placed it in his pocket. 'Now, gentlemen,' he said, 'you have already proved yourselves friends of the hospital, and I know you will not be prepared to stand by and let this happen. What I'd like to do is ask for suggestions from the floor as to what action we should take.'

Sydney Roper was first to his feet. 'I served in Italy during the war and saw what they did to Mussolini,' he said in a strong Cockney accent. 'Strung him up, they did, and left him dangling by his 'eels from a lamppost. My suggestion is that we 'ang the Mayor up by his chain from a lamppost outside the Town 'all.'

The sound of supportive applause came from a darkened corner at the back of the room. Everybody turned and peered into the gloom to find Matilda Thrush sitting alongside Nurse May and clapping her hands together enthusiastically.

Kilmore waved them forward, and as they moved to a seat in the front row Dr Tinkle came from his place on stage to join them. He kissed each of them extravagantly on the hand, Continental style.

Nurse May giggled. 'Ooh, Doctor,' she said, 'I don't think you'd have done that if you'd seen me working in the haemorrhoids ward an hour ago.'

Tinkle grimaced, and wiped his hand down the side of his trousers.

'This, as you all know, is Nurse May,' Kilmore announced, 'and with her a brave young lady who must remain anonymous.'

'You've got the wrong day, my dear,' said Francis Bigger. 'This is where I come for my AA meetings.'

Kilmore waited for the laughter to finish. 'It is thanks solely to her that we have advance knowledge of the Mayor's dastardly plans,' he explained. 'I will not name her because it's important to keep her identity secret. Let's just call her our Lady with the Lump.'

'I don't quite follow,' said Tinkle. 'Why lump?'

'The Mayor,' explained Kilmore, 'is the Lump.'

'Well, lady, you obviously approved of my action plan,' Sydney Roper said. 'Hang the big Lump from the lamppost.'

'I thought it was a wonderfully inventive idea,' said Matilda, 'but you refrained from saying by which part of his anatomy he would hang. I do hope you had his testicles in mind.'

The eyes of grown men watered as they envisaged the scene. 'Blimey, it would give a whole new meaning to the Mayor's ball and chain,' said Roper.

'It would be a suspended sentence,' added Biddle.

Kilmore wiped his eyes with his handkerchief, and then called the meeting to order. 'Thank you for that contribution, Sydney, and for the lady's seconding motion,' he said. 'Now do we have any suggestions for a less, um, drastic solution?'

'Oooh, yes, I've got a heaven-sent idea,' offered 'The Right Reverend' Francis Bigger. 'Let's have a prayer meeting at Wembley Stadium, and pray for the deliverance of the hospital. We could attract thousands of punters, I mean pilgrims, by telling them that the end is nigh.'

'You can pray for my deliverance first,' said Charlie Baron. 'I think it's triplets this time.'

'Now listen to Francis,' Bigger demanded. 'Just think how much we could collect towards my, I mean the hospital funds. You'd be amazed, I can tell you.'

He was now on his feet and in full voice. 'Gather ye round brothers and sisters and hear me,' he shouted at full volume, his arms raised to the heavens. 'Don't let mine be a voice in the wilderness. Remember what the Good Book sayeth, "Give and I will receive." Listen, listen to Francis of Ah's-easy. I pray, you pay. Just put your money where my mouth is.'

Kilmore tried hard not to look too astonished. 'Uh, quite, Reverend Francis,' he said. 'We'll obviously bear your kind money-raising offer in mind. Any other suggestions?'

'How about kidnapping the Mayor?' said Bernie Biddle. 'Hold him to ransom. The Mayor for the future of the hospital.'

'There's one major weakness with that plan,' Matilda said with feeling. 'There's every likelihood that the Council would not want the Mayor back. In fact I am certain they would be prepared to sacrifice the hospital rather than negotiate his freedom.'

Local market stallholders Peter Smith and Fred Apple

had most to lose if a supermarket were to open on their territory. They would not only lose their hospital but also much of their custom. Peter Smith stood. 'I want to set out our stall for both of us,' he said. 'Juicy and I have talked this through, and we think the only answer is to have a leak.'

'The lavatory's downstairs by the public bar,' said Bernie Biddle.

'No, I mean leak the letter,' said Smith. 'Let the local *Mercury* have it so that they can show up the Mayor for the conniving crook that he is.'

'We did consider this,' said Kilmore. 'But you've heard what's in the letter. There's not a jury in the country that would believe anybody could be stupid enough to send a letter like this. The Mayor will just deny it, and then sue the hospital for thousands for defamation.'

Kilmore looked around the room to see if there were any more suggestions. None were forthcoming. 'The way I see it, ladies and gentlemen, is there are *two* people we should tackle,' he said. 'The Mayor, of course, could become the direct target, but first on our hit list should be Percy Dick, the health and safety inspector. We know that he's in on this scam. What we don't know is when he's going to make his inspection. If you're willing, I would like to set up a rota so that we all take turns watching for him to arrive at the hospital. Our Lady will provide a photograph so that we know exactly who we're looking out for.'

'We already know him,' said Sydney Roper. 'He's the geezer who came to investigate our complaints about the hospital grub. Tall skinny bloke with a terrible squint.'

'I know who you mean,' said Bernie Biddle. 'When he looks at you he's really looking at the person next to you.'

'When he looks at me,' said Nurse May, 'I don't know which one he's looking at either.'

'He's looking at both of them,' said Fred Apple.

'You've got the right geezer,' said Sydney, punching his right fist into the open palm of his left hand. 'Cross-eyed git.'

'Well he'll be easy to identify,' said Kilmore. 'What we must do is make sure that in his role as health and safety inspector he submits an extremely favourable report that provides no reason whatsoever for the Mayor to push forward with his plan for knocking down the hospital. If that fails, we'll turn our attention on the Mayor himself. I've got a last ditch idea how we can make him change his mind, but first we must give Mr Percy Dick the treatment. I shall be in touch with you all with a look-out rota.'

Bernie Biddle put up his hand. 'Oi, Doc, what about the night shift. Are you going to provide a bed?'

'I'm sure that if there's an empty bed to have, Nurse May here will find it for you,' Kilmore said, quite innocently.

There was loud laughter and wolf whistles when Nurse May added: 'Well I always manage to find one for you, darling.'

'Even in the daytime I'll need the use of a bed,' said Baron, rubbing the small of his back. 'I'm suffering terribly from backache at the moment. I'm at least eight months into this pregnancy.'

'You'll have somewhere to rest,' said Nurse May. 'I'll have a word with Clarence. He'll fix you up.'

'I'm afraid that's not such a good idea,' said Kilmore. 'We might need to call on Clarence's union support in the future, but for now I think it best that he is kept very much in the dark about our plans. He is too close to the Matron...'

'Close!' said Sydney Roper. 'Blimey, if he got much closer he'd be wearing her knickers.'

'And I hear it wouldn't be the first time,' added Biddle.

'She's got room for both of them,' said Francis Bigger. 'You'd be amazed at the size of them. Amazed. Billy Graham could hold a crusade in them.'

'It has been said that her knicker elastic could launch a rocket to the moon,' said Fred Apple.

'I think Clarence deserves a medal for taking her on,' added Peter Smith. 'Kissing her must be like kissing a great big pomegranate.'

'You're so right, but without the juice,' said Dr Tinkle, speaking from unforgettable firsthand experience. 'It was a week before I could feel my lips. Thought I'd never play the euphonium again.'

Kilmore held up his hands. 'All right, that's enough,' he said. 'We're not here to discuss Matron's underwear or her private and personal life. The point I'm trying to make is that if Clarence were to tell Matron what we're up to she would very quickly scupper the plan, and go down the official road. Then our hands would be tied by suffocating red tape.'

48

'Oooh, that sounds different,' said Nurse May. 'Must try it out one day.'

Kilmore continued as if he had not heard her. 'Once officialdom is on the case we would not have any say in the matter,' he explained. 'You can bet that the Mayor has got several bureaucrats in his pocket, and they would go along with anything that he asked in return for a few back-handers.'

'I'll give him a back-hander across the mush,' said Sydney Roper.

'I know you would, Sydney,' said Kilmore. 'But I want us to adopt the Gandhi approach.'

'As in Goosey Goosey Gander?' said Charlie Baron.

'No, he means that little feller who wore baby's nappies,' said Bernie Biddle.

'Yeah,' said Sydney. 'Used to be a cloakroom attendant – Mahhat-mahcoat.'

'Behave yourselves, lads,' said Kilmore. 'This is deadly serious. Gandhi got what he wanted by being a pacifist and refusing to go down the road towards violence.'

'You're right, Doc,' said Sydney. 'We'll pacify the Mayor, and *then* I'll thump him in the mush.'

Kilmore realised it was time to wind up the meeting. Certain members of the audience were obviously getting thirsty. 'For now,' he stressed, 'tell Clarence nothing. If he were to find out about the Mayor's plan he would have every hospital in the country on a strike footing, and that would just antagonise everybody and the National Health would collapse.'

He looked at his watch and yawned. 'Well it's past

my bedtime.'

There was a cackle of a laugh from Nurse May. 'Any time is bedtime for you,' she said, bringing the meeting to a disorderly conclusion.

Kilmore was concentrating so hard on formulating his plans that, quite understandably, he forgot the fairly minor fact that he was on a stage. He walked forward to talk to Dr Tinkle at the end of his speech, and was suddenly walking on air as he came to the edge of the stage.

Kilmore landed head first at the feet of Nurse May, knocking himself out cold. 'Blimey, he really 'as fallen for you,' said Sydney Roper.

'Quick, is there a doctor in the house?' shouted Bernie Biddle.

'I'll say a prayer for him, if you like,' said Francis Bigger. 'I'd only charge a quid. Special rates for doctors. They tend to lean towards atheism. Not good for business.'

And so it was that Dr Tinkle was propping up Dr Kilmore as they left the Crown and Anchor. Their exit just happened to coincide with the arrival of the Matron, carrying out her voluntary part-time work selling the *War Cry* for the Salvation Army.

She instantly recognised Dr Kilmore, and wondered at first when noticing his half-bared right leg if she had happened upon some strange Freemasonry ritual. But seeing the way his feet dragged as Dr Tinkle pulled him along she was left with the only possible conclusion that he was once again terribly inebriated.

Matron made a mental note to report the incident to

the hospital governors, and to point out the doctor's obvious and very worrying drink problem.

Dr Tinkle steered the semi-conscious Kilmore into the pub car park and propped him up against his black Morris Minor. As he took his hands off him to search for his keys, Kilmore pitched slowly forward like a puppet that has had its strings cut away and he finished resting on his chin with his bottom stuck up in the air. It was just as Tinkle bent down behind him to haul him back up that PC Shufflebottom walked into the car park on his regular look-out for drunken drivers. His six foot five inch frame cast a sudden shadow over the two locked together doctors.

'Gotcha, you bloody perverts,' he boomed, making Tinkle literally jump with shock.

'The Wolfenden Report states that consenting adults can only do it in the privacy of their own rooms,' Shufflebottom said, reaching for his pen and notebook. 'A pub car park is hardly private.'

'Don't be an imbecile, Constable,' Tinkle said. 'This man is ill and I'm a doctor.'

'The fact that you're a doctor don't give you the right to perform an unlawful and lewd act in public,' Shufflebottom pronounced, feeling the full power of his position. 'It is now incumbent on me to take down your particulars.'

'You'll never make it stick,' said Tinkle.

'I'm not interested in that sort of filthy talk,' said Shufflebottom. 'All I know is what I saw with me own two eyes, and you are right in it. Or you certainly nearly

51

were anyway.'

Kilmore had now come round, and got slowly and unsteadily to his feet. He was swaying against the driver's side of Tinkle's car.

Shufflebottom's eyes lit up as he recognised him. 'Oh, it's you,' he said. 'I might have guessed you were one of them. I will also be charging you with being drunk while showing intent to enter and drive a vehicle. That is an even more serious offence than having unlawful intimacy with a person what is of the same gender as what you are.'

'But this man has just had a nasty accident,' pleaded Tinkle.

'He would have done if I had not arrived in the nick of time,' said Shufflebottom. 'I must now ask both of you gentlemen to accompany me to the station where I will formally...'

His voice trailed away as his eye was captured by the unmistakable backside-wriggling, miniskirted walk of Nurse May. 'Her buttocks move like the arse of a thoroughbred racehorse in the paddock,' was how one of the boys at the station had so aptly described it, or them.

'What's up, Doc?' she said to Tinkle. 'Thought you were taking Jimmy back to his digs for a rest.'

Shufflebottom was blushing scarlet over the sudden and unexpected close proximity of the girl of his randy dreams.

'I found these two gentlemen at it, miss,' he said.
'At what?'
'At each other, miss. Right here in the car park of

this public house.'

'Get away,' said Nurse May. 'I can vouch for the fact that neither of these men has a single gay bone in their body.'

It was at that moment that the still dizzy Kilmore said, 'I feel quite queer.'

'See, miss,' said Shufflebottom. 'Admits it, he does. The man is a confessed pervert of the homosexual persuasion. It is my duty as an hofficer of the law to protect the public from such a man as what he is, begging your pardon miss.'

It was dawning on the still dazed Kilmore that they were in some sort of trouble with his old police adversary.

'What's the matter now, PC bloody Stinker?' he said, irritated by the thumping pain in his head. 'Why are you persecuting me?'

'Are you Stinker Shufflebottom?' asked Nurse May.

The constable nodded, his blush now a blaze.

Kilmore had told her about the bet down at the police station, and that Shufflebottom was desperate for a date.

The situation was suddenly tailor-made for Nurse May. She might not have been top of the class at the nursing college (she was the one who, when asked in the exam paper to describe the difference between a fly and a mosquito, wrote, 'Dunno, I've never unzipped a mosquito'), but she could have picked up an honours degree in the art of seduction.

She took Shufflebottom gently by the arm and steered him out of the earshot of the two doctors.

'I'll tell you what, Stinker... no I can't call you that,' she said in a stage whisper. 'What's your proper name?'

'PC Shufflebottom, miss.'

'No, what comes first, silly boy.'

'Three four double seven, miss.'

'Not your number, dopey. Your first name.'

' Simon, miss.'

'Thought it might be,' Nurse May said quietly to herself. 'Now then, Simon,' she said to the constable in her sexiest voice, 'why don't you and I discuss when we can have a little intimate rendezvous, while these two very tired and very dedicated doctors go off home. I'd love the chance to see your truncheon, and perhaps you'll be able to show me how your handcuffs work as well. Bet you know how to give a girl an arresting time, don't you darling?'

The car park resounded to her cackling laugh.

Shufflebottom tried hard to control the sudden shaking of his hands, but the pencil bouncing on the page was clear evidence of the effect Nurse May was having on him.

She squeezed his arm, and then got up on tip toe as she whispered as close to his ear as she could get. 'Of course,' she said, blowing hot air on to the constable's neck, 'I couldn't possibly make a date with you if you were involved in court action with doctors from my hospital. That would put us both in an impossible position, and believe me, darling, I know some impossible positions.'

The perspiring PC Shufflebottom was now feeling exceptionally hot under his collar. And it wasn't only his temperature that was rising.

He considered the size of the pot in the police station 'who'll-be-first-to-pull-the-nurse' bet, and then considered the size of her prize assets. He also weighed up the merit in taking two fairly respected doctors back to the station and trying to convince the duty sergeant that he had sufficient evidence to book them for buggery. It was no race.

He told the two doctors he was letting them off with just a warning, and took down Nurse May's particulars instead.

5

M AYOR COCKLEWELL was finding it more than some what disconcerting trying to have a covert face-to-face talk with Percy Dick when the health and safety inspector kept continually looking towards the far corner of his office. His eyes were so crossed that they virtually looked at each other.

'Why the hell don't you get your eyes seen to?' he blurted. 'You can go and get them done on the National 'ealth for nowt.'

'Why, what's wrong with them?' Dick replied testily, his right eye looking a yard-and-a-half to the left of him and the left eye looking just beyond the Mayor's right ear.

'What d'you mean what's wrong with them?' said the Mayor. 'Are you blind or something? Why, your eyes are more bloody crossed than a bishop's Bible.'

Dick laughed, revealing tobacco-stained teeth that were not the best advert for a health inspector. 'It's not my eyes that are wrongly adjusted,' he said. 'It's everybody elses. All you people who look straight ahead are the ones with the real problems. Did you know that statistics show that 99.9 per cent of road accidents are caused by people who can see straight? The roads would be a great deal safer if everybody was cross-eyed like me.'

The Mayor found it impossible to argue with such clear-eyed logic.

'But don't you get irritated not being able to look directly at the person that you're talking to?' he asked, trying hard to look him straight in the eyes.

'But I *am* looking directly at you,' Dick said, his eyes now trained twenty degrees to the right and left of the Mayor.

'But how do I know that?' asked Cocklewell, in a state of some exasperation.

'It's what I know and what I see that matters,' Dick explained patiently, like an optician discussing the need for spectacles. 'The positioning of my eyes are the greatest possible asset in my job. For instance, I was called to inspect the kitchen in a local hotel today following a complaint from a customer who had reported finding mice droppings on his plum duff. While the chef thought I was looking the other way during my inspection I distinctly saw him kicking a dead mouse under the refrigerator. Cost him a fiver to make me keep my mouth shut. All thanks to my eyes.'

The Mayor tried to look impressed. 'Well spotted, Dick,' he said.

'And now, for instance,' the health inspector continued, 'I appear to be looking at you when in actual fact I can see into the outer office where Miss Thrush is taking what I consider to be a rather unhealthy interest in our conversation.'

Matilda heard what he said, but showed no sign of being worried by his statement.

The Mayor was equally unconcerned. 'Don't worry about Tilly,' he said. 'She knows all my business. Perfectly trustworthy that one.'

57

He leant across his desk and added in a loud whisper, 'Y'see, she fancies me something rotten. I'm fighting it mind. She keeps making advances, but so far I've not given into temptation. Man in my position has got to be careful about where he puts his mayoral mace, if you follow my drift.'

The way Dick was looking past him Mayor Cocklewell was amazed he could follow anything, let alone his drift.

Matilda heard the whisper, and made a mental note to double that day's bromide dose.

'Reet, to get down t'brass tacks,' the Mayor said, lighting a giant cigar. He blew the smoke towards the wall, and Dick rubbed his eyes.

'Reason I've called you in today is t'prime you for a very important inspection job that has to have a certain incontestable conclusion.'

'Are we talking fleapit cinema type of conclusion?' asked Dick.

'Exactly, Percy,' the Mayor said, beaming. 'You might not be able to see straight but there's nowt wrong with your powers of perception. But this is a bigger job, and so therefore a bigger brown envelope. We're talking two hundred smackers here.'

Dick smiled the smile of greed at the Mayor as he looked at the wall. 'Two hundred,' he said. 'That's the equivalent of six weeks' wages, so it must be a big place you want closed down. What's the target?'

''aven 'ospital.'

The health inspector was so startled that his eyes swivelled. 'But that place is my bread and butter,' he said. 'Where would I be as a health inspector without a hospital to inspect? And it's one of my pleasures in life to be able to go there and ogle at the nurses without them knowing it. There's a Nurse May there. Cor! You should see her knockers. They're enough to make you go boss-eyed. So what consolation is there for me if the hospital closes down?'

'I've thought of that,' said the Mayor. 'If you can produce a report that 'elps me get the 'ospital closed I'll see to it that you're promoted to roads and 'ighways inspector. Lots of brown envelope possibilities in that department.'

The Mayor tried to be funny. 'I'm sure you'd find t'crossroads quite a challenge,' he said.

Dick did not even begin to see the joke. All he could see was Miss Thrush scribbling down copious notes as they talked.

'You're absolutely sure that Miss Thrush can be trusted?' he asked quietly, looking over the Mayor's shoulder.

The Mayor fought the impulse to look behind him. 'Of course she can.'

'But she appears to be noting down every word that we're saying.'

'That's quite reet and very observant of you considering your, um, eye 'andicap,' said the Mayor, clenching the cigar between his teeth. 'It's what we privately and confidentially call "Operation White House". You probably don't know this, but all the American Presidents have their conversations noted down for reasons of historical record.'

59

Dick shook his head as his gaze wandered to the wall where he saw the Mayor puffing new life into his cigar. 'That sounds a dangerous thing to do to me,' he said. 'Strikes me a President could land himself in trouble doing that. There are some things that should never be overheard.'

'No problem,' said the Mayor. 'If there were ever any hint of an inquiry, you just get your secretary to erase the incriminating passages. It's amazing what you can do with a rubber.'

Dick moved uncomfortably on his seat. 'But how do I know you're not going to incriminate me?' he said, looking towards the window for a better view of Miss Thrush. 'If you've got a note of the fact that I've agreed to help close down the hospital, I'd be up to my eyes in it.'

The Mayor laughed out loud. 'That's a good 'un, that one is, Percy. Up to your eyes in it. I'm sure that would make you very cross.'

Dick was not amused. 'I'm still not happy about it,' he said. 'I cannot understand why you should allow Miss Thrush to overhear everything we say.'

'I promise you that you're worrying yourself over absolutely nowt,' said the Mayor. 'It's just that I want a complete record of all that I achieve during my year of office. For prosperity, and for profit. It will help me write my memoirs.'

'Your memoirs?' said Dick.

'Aye, that's reet,' said the Mayor. 'It will be the inside story about being a mayor in a busy metropolitan district that I have turned into a gold mine for local industry. I shall call it Metro Golden Mayor.'

Dick looked directly at Mayor Cocklewell and said to the wall: 'I think Carry On Mayor would be a more appropriate title.'

Matilda lay beside Dr Tinkle in the digs he shared with Dr Kilmore, giving him a full report of the meeting between Cocklewell and the health inspector.

'When is he due to make the inspection?' asked Tinkle, just getting his breath back after a love session that made nonsense of rumours that Matilda would be happy to see all men castrated.

'The Mayor left it to the inspector to decide,' she said. 'The only thing he stressed was that he wanted a damning report on his desk within a week.'

'Ooh, that wicked, wicked Mayor,' said Tinkle. 'I shall tell Dr Strangelove to set up the inspector-watch rota first thing tomorrow.'

'Dr Strangelove?' said Matilda.

'That's what I call Jimmy Kilmore,' he explained. 'Believe me, he's made love to some very strange women in his time, and in some very strange places.'

'Such as?'

'Would you believe that I once caught him with a nurse on the roofrack of my Morris Minor. When I asked what he was doing up there, he replied, "I'm just proving to this young lady that I am very good at Morris dancing."'

'He seems very smitten with this Nurse May,' Matilda said.

'Yes,' agreed Tinkle. 'I've never known him get so

61

serious before. Jealous even. He's a bundle of nerves over the date she's made for this evening with PC Shufflebottom. She only did it to get us out of trouble. Now she's lumbered with going to the pictures with him to help him win his bet. Kilmore has promised her that he's got a plan to get her off the hook.'

Matilda swung her legs out of bed. 'I must go for a tinkle, Tinkle,' she said. 'When I come back, you can make me twinkle, Tinkle.'

As she disappeared into the bathroom, the doctor lay back wondering how Kilmore was getting on with what he had dubbed his 'Nurse May-Day' rescue plan.

Kilmore wore a belted white mac with the collar turned up and a trilby with the brim pulled down low over his eyes as he followed Nurse May on the way to the Odeon cinema in the town centre. To further disguise himself he had a drooping Mexican-style moustache glued beneath his nose.

He wanted to keep a close surveillance so that he could react instantly if Stinker Shufflebottom tried to go too far with her. Nurse May had no idea that he was on her trail. He did not want her to think that he was becoming too attached to her, but he knew from the way his heart was racing that she was the first woman to arouse his emotions as well as his sexual appetite.

Just as he rounded the corner into the road where the cinema was located a stray dog was loping contentedly away from a steaming packet that it had deposited on the pavement. There are those who will tell you that what was about to happen to Dr Kilmore is lucky, but no doubt he would dispute this old wives' tale. He was so intent on looking ahead to the wriggling behind of Nurse May that he did not spot the brown mound, and his leading right foot came down straight into the soft centre.

Kilmore skidded several yards until his forward projection was stopped by the immoveable obstruction of a lamppost. He hammered into it shoulder first, and at least had the consolation of it not connecting with his face and further damaging his still bruised and painful nose.

As he attempted to scrape the cloying brown mess from his shoe by rubbing it against the edge of the curb, a drunken on-leave sailor came walking on an unsteady path around the same corner and took the same path through the dog's muck. He too ended up wrapped around the lamppost.

Kilmore pointed at what was left of the brown heap and uttered the immortal words, 'I just did that.'

The drunken sailor was sober enough to see his target. He pulled back his right fist and then slammed it forward on to the bridge of Kilmore's nose, sending his moustache spinning clockwise until what had been a drooping Mexican style was now of the handlebar variety. 'Dirty git,' the sailor said, as he rubbed the doctor's face in the ruins of the dog's mountainous pile.

Kilmore cleaned himself up as best he could with what was once a white handkerchief, and then continued his pursuit of Nurse May.

He knew that by now she would be inside the cinema with Stinker Shufflebottom, a nickname that could at that moment hang very well on Kilmore as he and the stench of the dog turned into the Odeon foyer.

The doctor bought a three-and-ninepenny ticket for the stalls, and wondered how he would be able to spot Shufflebottom and Nurse May in the dark. He need not have worried. As soon as he reached the centre aisle he was able to make out the unmistakeable giant silhouette of the constable. He was sat four rows from the back, and as if to make identification just a little easier he was still wearing his helmet.

What Kilmore was not to know is that seated in the row immediately behind Shufflebottom were four of his police colleagues, all in plain clothes. They were there to witness the date. The bet was that not only did he have to take Nurse May out but that he should be seen to get a kiss from her. Otherwise all bets were off.

Kilmore pulled his trilby even lower over his eyes, and then, with the usherette's torch to guide him, pushed his way into the row behind Shufflebottom and Nurse May. All eyes in the immediate vicinity turned as the picturegoers got his scent. The brim of the trilby and the Salvador Dali upward sweep of the moustache protected his identity, but if necessary he would be easily identified by his smell.

He sat down directly behind PC Shufflebottom, with the constable's colleagues either side of him. The film was *And God Created Woman,* an erotic film starring a sex kitten called Brigitte Bardot. With the obstruction of Shufflebottom's helmet Kilmore could not see the screen and neither could he follow the dialogue. He sat intently watching the constable and Nurse May to detect any signs of improper movement.

Kilmore could tell from the change of the background music to a romantic theme and the sudden heavy breathing that things were hotting up on the screen. As he had sensed, Shufflebottom used this sexually-charged moment to make his move.

He slowly slipped an arm around Nurse May, and as he bent forward to kiss her Kilmore suddenly produced a smoke canister from his mac pocket and, pulling the release button, rolled it under Shufflebottom's seat. As smoke billowed around the constable and the nurse, the four plain clothes policemen stood at the same time as Kilmore and shouted, 'Fire!' They were delighted to have this unexpected chance to save their bet.

There was pandemonium as everybody in the audience started to dash for the emergency exits. Shufflebottom did his policeman's duty and helped shepherd people out into the street.

The fire brigade arrived in a matter of minutes, mainly because their station was right next door to the cinema and also because half the force were inside watching Shufflebottom's progress with Nurse May. They, too, were in on the bet.

Kilmore was still sitting crouched forward in his seat trying to retrieve the canister when a hose was turned on from the aisle. He was suddenly hit by a powerful jet of water that lifted him out of his seat. His trilby hat and moustache went soaring up into the circle, landing on a worse-for-drink on-leave sailor who had been snoozing through the film.

Soaking wet, Kilmore made his way to the cinema

toilet and dried off as best he could. By the time he re-emerged the canister had been found and the film was back on the screen. He knew he dare not go back to his seat because Shufflebottom would recognise him without his hat and moustache. Suddenly he had a brainwave, and dashed out of the exit and up the stairs. On the second landing he came to a door marked PRIVATE. PROJECTIONISTS ONLY.

PC Shufflebottom had by now returned to his seat with Nurse May, and was again waiting for the right moment to claim his kiss when on to the screen a notice flashed up across Brigitte Bardot's bared breasts: WOULD NURSE MAY PLEASE REPORT FOR DUTY TO HAVEN HOSPITAL IMMEDIATELY.

The four plain clothes policemen and half a dozen off-duty firemen read the notice aloud in unison, just in case Shufflebottom had missed it. Upstairs in the circle a drunken sailor was awakened by the chanting from downstairs, and instinctively responded with: 'Amen'.

A relieved Nurse May got quickly to her feet. 'Sorry, Simon, but I must rush,' she said. 'Duty calls. You stay and watch the rest of the film. Thanks for a very lov... uh, a very eventful evening.'

She bent forward and gave the constable a light kiss on the cheek.

Shufflebottom roared like a football fan celebrating a winning goal at Wembley. His four colleagues and the firemen released a chorus of groans and curses.

On the screen Brigitte Bardot gave a coy smile and covered her bare breasts with her folded arms.

In the projectionist's room, Kilmore smiled. The crisp

66

pound note now in the palm of the projectionist could be considered money well spent.

Upstairs in the circle a worse-for-drink on-leave sailor got the shock of his life. He looked into the toilet room mirror to discover that while asleep during the film he had grown a moustache.

The London evening newspapers the next day carried an identikit of a man the police were seeking for causing a disturbance at the Odeon cinema.

Nurse May sat up in bed alongside Dr Kilmore in his digs staring at the artist's impression. She turned the paper round, and looked at the picture from several angles. 'D'you know something, Jimmy,' she said, 'I'd swear that was you if it wasn't for the handlebar moustache.'

Police were later reported to have interviewed an on-leave sailor who had been sitting in the circle at the time of the fire. He fitted the description of the wanted man, down to the trilby and also a moustache that the police found to be false.

He told the police: 'I always thought it brought you luck if you trod in dog's muck.'

6

THE RIGHT REVEREND Francis Bigger was in full flow with his evangelistic message at the local concert hall. 'Listen,' he said to his congregation of a scattering of pensioners looking for a place out of the cold, a group of young pop fans who had decided to take their places twenty-four hours early for a Beatles concert, and two planted 'disciples' who were paid to be there. 'Listen to Francis. I come here today with a message of hope from Matthew, Mark, Luke and John...'

'What about Paul, George and Ringo?' a young Mersey girl shouted.

'Them 'n' all,' said Bigger, whose knowledge of pop music had not yet even reached the Gracie Fields era.

'I stand here as testimony of the miracles of the Lord.'

'Hallelujah, he's saved!' yelled the plump, bespectacled lady sitting on the stage alongside him shaking a tambourine.

'Not yet, you deaf old bat,' Bigger said out of the corner of his mouth.

He glanced at her and winced. 'Why, dear Lord,' he said in silent supplication, 'did you lumber me with her? Of all the women on this earth I land her as a wife. I know that you work your miracles in mysterious ways, oh Lord, but I'm blowed if I can find what's so special about this one.'

Bigger sensed that he was losing his audience, and returned to the main thrust of his address. 'For me to carry on the Lord's good deeds here on earth I unfortunately need that which is not easily forthcoming,' he said. 'I refer, of course, to bread... as in dough... as in moolah... readies... spondulicks. When the Good Lord spared me from imminent death in the great Haven Hospital a short-time ago doctors were astonished by my recovery. Nay, and thrice nay, they were amazed.'

'Hallelujah, he's saved,' Mrs Bigger shouted, with another shake of her tambourine.

'You're still coming in too early,' Bigger growled. 'Wait for your cue, you silly cow.'

He looked down at his audience, and silently implored their attention with a doleful look of his eyes that he had practised for hours on end in the mirror. 'I was given just forty-eight hours to live, my brothers and sisters,' he said, his voice shaking with forced emotion. 'That's right. Two days. In just forty-eight hours Francis would have been a goner. Kaput. Defunct. Departed. Dead. No more. My toes were all ready to curl up when the Good Lord above intervened. "Francis," he said in a booming voice, "we're not yet ready for you. There is still much for you to do here on earth, carrying on my work and spreading my word."'

Bigger raised his arms to the heavens as he approached his most dramatic bit. 'With that there was a clap of thunder...'

He waited for his wife to crash her tambourine.

Nothing.

' ...There was a clap of thunder,' he shouted.

Nothing.

He looked down to find Mrs Bigger slumped in her upright chair fast asleep, her silent tambourine on her lap.

He now shouted at the top of his voice, this time looking away from the audience and aiming his words directly at his wife.

'There was a great bloody clap of thunder!' he roared.

Mrs Bigger was startled into action. 'Hallelujah, he's saved,' she shouted.

'Not that bit yet,' Bigger shouted. 'The tambourine. The clap of thunder.'

Mrs Bigger feebly shook her tambourine, and her husband offered up a silent prayer for forgiveness for what he was thinking of doing to her when this meeting was over.

'As the thunder clapped, the skies opened and I was drawn up from my death-bed as if by a magnet,' he said, his full-volume voice booming around the largely empty concert hall. 'Doctors had prophesised that I would never leave my bed again, except in a wooden overcoat. But there I was standing, and ready to do the Lord's work...'

He waited for his wife's hallelujah call, but she had nodded off again.

One of the plants in the audience realised a supporting response was needed, and made a contribution that was somewhat lacking rehearsed polish and perfection. 'Hallelujah,' he shouted. 'He's been paid.'

Bigger looked to the heavens, his face turning purple

with what he hoped was hidden rage. As he looked down he saw a familiar figure walking towards the stage from the main entrance. It was Sydney Roper.

'And, miracle of miracles, brothers and sisters, here appearing from nowhere is a man who was a witness to me rising from the dead.'

He pointed dramatically in the direction of Roper, who looked over his shoulder to see who he was pointing at. When he realised it was him he ducked into the nearest seat, wishing himself invisible.

Bigger brought his voice down a few decibels. This unexpected chance to verify his story needed gentle communication. The greater the lie, the greater the volume was his motto.

'Brother Sydney Roper,' he said, trying desperately to force a tear. 'You yourself were also spared from death at the same time as me...'

Roper squirmed in his seat. 'I had an ingrowing toenail,' he said.

'True, true, you brave man,' Bigger said, 'but you are keeping it from this blessed congregation that it had turned septic.'

'That is correct,' said Roper. 'Hurt like bleedin' hell, it did.'

Bigger was now back in full flow. 'There you have it from the mouth of the man himself. It hurt like hell. But he was spared that place in hell so that he can one day take his place in heaven. Tell them, Brother Sydney, how you saw me just forty-eight hours away from extinction.'

'The 'ospital gave you two days notice. I remember

it well. You overheard them saying you had forty-eight hours left and you took that to mean you had just a couple of days left before you kicked the bucket...'

Bigger interrupted before Roper spilled the beans that he had forty-eight hours to get out of hospital so that his bed could go to a genuinely sick patient.

'That's right, Brother,' he shouted. 'Very colourfully put. I had just forty-eight hours before I kicked the bucket. But then I was saved, and am now spreading the Lord's word.'

Bigger realised he had at last moved his congregation when the crowd of young schoolgirls at the back of the hall started to sing, 'She loves you, yeah, yeah, yeah.'

He was moved almost to tears. 'Sing my children,' he shouted. 'Praise the lord.'

They should, of course, have been singing 'He' loves you, but he decided to make allowances. This was obviously all to do with that women's lib business he had heard was sweeping America.

'While our children's choir are rejoicing, my good lady wife, Sister Enid, will now pass among you with her tambourine at the ready,' he announced. 'Any contributions placed in it will be most gratefully received. Oh yes, most gratefully. Please, please don't worry if you have no money to donate.'

He gave as close as he could to a hollow laugh. 'It is not as if Francis will strike you down with a streak of lightning if you do not cough up,' he said, doing his best to make it sound like a threat.

As his wife moved among the widely scattered audience, Roper came on stage. 'We've been tipped off that the 'ealth inspector is due at the 'ospital any time in the next few days,' he said. 'What rota shift can I put you down for?'

'The night-shift, please,' Bigger said, almost pleading. 'Anything to get me away from her snoring. Sounds like an old sow with her snout stuck in a wind tunnel.'

They were joined by Mrs Bigger who had finished the collection. Roper was impressed to see two half crowns gleaming inside the tambourine. There were also an assortment of buttons, some chewing gum and a Beatles badge.

'Five bob ain't bad,' said Roper. 'Blimey, that's more than most of my betting shop punters earn in an hour.'

Bigger's face was as black as thunder. 'That's as maybe,' he said, 'but I've been up here rabbiting on for more than two hours. My throat's as dry as Lawrence of Arabia's saddle.'

'Even so,' said Roper, 'five bob ain't a bad take from a congregation this small. Blimey, I've seen more people in a telephone kiosk.'

Bigger picked up the two half crowns. 'This money,' he said, 'is mine. It's what I gave the plants to place in the tambourine as encouragement and an example for all the others. Tight-fisted miseries. Try to save their souls and what thanks do I get? Everybody wants something for nothing these days. I can't wait to get back into hospital for a relief from all this.'

The girls' choir was now in full voice. 'But, Brother Sydney, I do have my consolations,' Bigger said, pointing at the small army of schoolgirls waving their banners and dancing at the back of the hall. 'Just look at the way I have reached out and touched these young ladies with my message. That is as satisfying as money. Well almost. They came in here looking for something special, and, verily, verily, Francis has given it to them.'

He had to confess that 'I Want to Hold Your Hand' was not a hymn with which he was familiar. And who were these prophets John, Paul, George and Ringo?

Bernie Biddle laughed out loud at the memory of Dr Kilmore walking on air as he came off the stage. It was one of the funniest sights he had seen in months. He laughed again as he conjured up a mental image of the way the doctor had landed nose first in front of Nurse May. Tears rolled down his cheeks. There was only one slight problem with the way Bernie was laughing and clearly enjoying himself. He just happened to be on duty driving a hearse in his undertaking role.

Funeral director Ivor Bodie, resplendent in top hat and tails and flourishing a silver-topped cane, walked on ahead at funereal pace, his chest pumped with pride at the reaction his cortege was drawing from passers-by. He had not realised that Mrs Murgatroyd, the 83-year-old widow he was preparing to commit to the ground, was so popular. People were stopping and pointing, and were clearly moved at the sight of the two-car procession as he led it through the high street at snail's pace.

Usually he would get impatient motorists behind tooting their horns, but today he sensed a spirit of true mourning and respect in the air. It gave him an uplifting feeling to know that people could still find it in their hearts to be sad. Trouble with the world today, he thought, was there was not enough misery around. People were having too good a time and getting fitter and healthier, and he didn't like it one bit. It was not like in the good old days forty years ago when he used to be able to hand out his calling card that carried the inspired message, 'If you've got a good cough, I've got a good coffin to carry you off in.'

But the increasingly good health of people since that damned Aneurin Bevin had introduced the National Health Act in 1948 had been a severe blow to his profession, and if it continued like this it could be the death of his business. For a brief second there, Bodie thought he overheard a deep-throated chuckle behind him. But it must have been a trick of the wind.

Bodie glanced over his shoulder at his new hearse driver Bernie Biddle, and saw that he was wiping tears from his eyes. This show of emotion was beyond the call of duty, and he made a mental note to give him a substantial rise. At least another tanner an hour. Well, maybe not quite so generous. Bodie would settle for offering a threepenny bit extra.

A bystander suddenly stepped into the road and started walking alongside the hearse. It astonished Bodie, who wondered if it was going to develop into one of those Egyptian-style funerals that he had seen on the newsreel at the picture house, with thousands of people trying to touch the coffin. 'Stay back you dirty Arab,' he shouted over his shoulder. 'Nobody gets their mitts on one of my coffins.'

Sydney Roper, for it was he, waved to the funeral

director. 'It's all right, guv'nor,' he called. 'Just paying me last respects. He was a lovely geezer.'

Bodie bit his tongue. 'Lovely geezer?' he thought. 'I didn't know Mrs Murgatroyd went in for that cross-dressing lark. If I'd have known that I would have recommended a cremation. Burn the old witch.'

Biddle signalled for Sydney to jump into the passenger seat alongside him. 'What's up, mate?' he asked. 'You didn't know the old dear, did you?'

'What old dear's that?'

'The one in the back.'

Sydney looked back at the coffin.

'How do I know? The lid's down. Might have known 'er. What did she do before she died?'

Bernie's brow furrowed. 'The usual, I suppose,' he said. 'Went white, coughed a couple of times and then croaked.'

'No, knucklehead, I mean what did she do for a living?'

'She was a widow.'

'That's not much of a living. Pension's lousy.'

'So what's so important Syd that it can't wait for us to get our client into the ground?'

'It's the 'ealth inspector,' said Sydney. 'He's due any day now and we've got to get the rota system working. Would you mind doing nights with Francis?'

''Course not,' said Bernie. 'I like hospitals at night. They're nearly as peaceful as a graveyard.'

Ivor Bodie dramatically held up his cane to call the cortege to a halt directly opposite the Crown and Anchor. He was sure Mrs Murgatroyd must have had an occasional gin and orange in the snug in her youth, and so it was only right and proper that he should briefly stop here while patrons paid their last respects. It also gave him time to nip in for a quick snifter.

The one problem was that Bernie Biddle was so engrossed in conversation with Sydney that he did not see Bodie signal that he was off for some refreshment. He continued to drive, gradually picking up speed while chatting away and forgetting that he was driving a hearse. He had gone more than a mile when he realised the funeral director was no longer leading the way. A sudden chill gripped his heart. "'ere, Sydney,' he said in a panic, 'you didn't see me run over a geezer in a black top hat, did you?'

"'Course you didn't,' said Sydney. 'Would have felt him go under the wheels. You must have overtaken him. Not surprising the speed he was walking. Anybody would think he was going to a funeral.'

Bernie looked behind to find that he had lost the following car, and wondered what he should do next.

'Bloody hell,' he said. 'I'm lost. You got any idea where the cemetery is?'

Sydney shrugged. 'Search me, mate,' he said. 'I keep clear of them places. Give me the creeps, they do. You'll have to stop and ask the way.'

Up ahead, Bernie was relieved to spot a policeman on traffic duty. He would not have been quite so relieved had he known that it was PC Shufflebottom.

Bernie drew up alongside him. 'Excuse me, officer,' he said, 'but do you know where the cemetery is?'

Shufflebottom, his arms open wide to stop oncoming

traffic, looked at him suspiciously.

'That's an odd thing for a man driving a hearse to ask,' he said. 'What's going on, eh?'

'I've got this delivery to make,' Bernie said, indicating the coffin behind him with a nod of the head.

'What proof have you got that this vehicle is yours?' Shufflebottom asked. 'There's something fishy going on here.'

'Does he look like a bloke that would nick an 'earse?' said Sydney.

'As you happen to mention it, the answer is "yes",' said the constable, who prided himself on his powers of instinct. 'I want you to tell me the registration number of this vehicle.'

'D-E-D one,' said Bernie.

Shufflebottom checked. 'You're wrong,' he said. 'It's D-E-D two.'

'Blast,' said Bernie. 'I normally drive the following car. That's number one.'

'And pray, where is the following car?' asked Shufflebottom in his best Sherlock Holmes manner.

'I've, uh, lost it,' admitted Bernie.

The constable, whose arms were now beginning to get tired, sensed that he was on to something big here. 'Let me see if I understand you correctly, sir,' he said. 'You have not only lost the cemetery but also the funeral car that was following you?'

Shufflebottom ignored the growing cacophony of car horns being pressed by irate drivers increasingly irritated by the sight of his widespread arms.

'I think you'd better pull over here while I investigate

this matter further,' he said.

He dropped his arms to indicate where Bernie should park and both sets of traffic that he had been holding up took this as a signal to move off. There was the sound of metal hitting metal and glass headlights shattering as cars heading for the same stretch of road collided.

PC Shufflebottom shook his head as he surveyed the mayhem. 'Today's drivers,' he said. 'They've got no patience, that's their problem.'

He signalled for Bernie to open the back of the hearse. 'Right you,' he ordered Sydney, 'help him get that coffin out on to the pavement. I can smell smugglers a mile off. You're not fooling me. I've got a nose for this sort of thing.'

'You're taking a dead liberty here,' said Sydney.

'Mrs Murgatroyd won't be pleased,' said Bernie.

'Who's Mrs Murgatroyd?' Sydney and Shufflebottom asked in unison.

'She's the occupant of the box,' said Bernie.

'Come on, stop stalling' said the constable. 'Open the box.'

'I'd rather take the money,' said Sydney.

'Don't get funny with me,' said Shufflebottom. 'I want that box opened. Now.'

'All right, all right, keep your lid on,' said Bernie as he prised open the coffin with a crowbar taken from the hearse tool bag.

Penny-pinching Ivor Bodie had squashed the considerably large figure of Mrs Murgatroyd into a box a size too small. The shroud in which she had been wrapped while in his chapel of rest had become caught on the lid and as it was pulled open the deceased Mrs Murgatroyd sat up with it.

Bernie and Sydney jumped back a pace. PC Shufflebottom collapsed on to the pavement in a dead faint.

At that moment there was a squeal of tyres as the following funeral car careered around the corner and skidded to a halt alongside the coffin. Bodie, who had come dashing out of the pub shouting, 'Follow that hearse', leapt from the front passenger seat almost frothing at the mouth.

He charged towards Bernie and Sydney, waving his cane in the air and letting out a stream of invective that was not quite in keeping with the air of dignity and respectability that he liked to bring to his funerals. Seeing Mrs Murgatroyd sitting up and staring in his direction with a look of disapproval on her face, Bodie pulled back from administering physical violence. 'I beg your pardon, ma'am,' he said, doffing his top hat. 'I should not use language like that in the hearing of good ladies like yourself.'

He then turned to Bernie and Sydney and started to roar again, but this time without the blue-coloured adjectives. 'What d'you think you're doing with my client?' he demanded, waving the cane to indicate Mrs Murgatroyd. 'You're a pair of bloody body snatchers, you are. Burke and Hare.'

Sydney's fright at the sight of Mrs Murgatroyd rising up in her box had now given way to hysterical laughter. 'You're the berk,' he said to the funeral director. 'Fancy losing a body on the way to the cemetery.'

Now Bernie was also laughing as he struggled to push the stiffer than stiff Mrs Murgatroyd back into the box.

Bodie used his cane for a shoehorn effect, and they managed to ease the body back under the lid.

'Right, Biddle,' he said, 'that's the last funeral you'll attend until your own. I'll make it my business to see to it that no other undertaker in the country will employ you. I'll have you blackballed.'

Sydney winced. 'That's a bit strong, guv'nor,' he said. 'Bernie doesn't deserve to have his privates blackened. He was only doing his job.'

They were joined from the funeral car by a middle-aged mourner dressed all in black. She was lifting a veil from her face and wiping her eyes with a white lace handkerchief.

'I'm just sorting it out, Miss Murgatroyd,' Bodie said, giving a passable impersonation of Uriah Heep. 'We'll soon have your mother in her rightful resting place. Rest on me.'

PC Shufflebottom had now come round, and was trying desperately to understand what was going on.

He got hold of Bernie by the arms and forced him back against the hearse. 'I'm arresting you for suspected kidnap and driving a hearse with undue care and attention,' he said. 'You've not only lost your job but also your freedom. You'll get at least six years for this. Nicking a body what is dead is a very serious offence in the heyes of the law.'

'Take your hands off him at once, Constable,' said Miss Murgatroyd, still dabbing away at her eyes.

'But he has caused you and your mother what is deceased great haggravation and hanxiety, Miss,' said the constable. 'I can tell from your tears that you are obviously suffering enormous distress.'

'These are tears of laughter that I'm wiping away,' said Miss Murgatroyd, 'and I'm here to tell you that this man has done no wrong whatsoever. In fact he has just given my mother more excitement than she has ever known before. She always regretted not having any adventure, but now she's found out just what fun it can be.'

She watched as Bernie and Sydney lifted the coffin and pushed it back into the hearse. 'This,' she said, 'has been the most memorable day of mother's life.'

7

ONLY IN HINDSIGHT was there any reason why Dr Kilmore should have considered it necessary to dwell on the odds of there being *two* tall, skinny squint-eyed men calling at the hospital, both of them with the prefix 'Inspector' in front of their name.

'Ah, Inspector,' he said in greeting as he spotted the man accurately answering the description of Percy Dick come through the main entrance. 'We've been expecting you. Welcome to Haven Hospital, the cleanest, healthiest and most efficiently run hospital in the entire country.'

The Inspector looked either side and across Kilmore at one and the same time. 'I was not aware that anybody knew I was coming,' he said. 'This is not my usual route.'

'Oh yes,' Kilmore said, 'We were given fair warning. It will be my pleasure to take you on a personal guided tour.'

'A tour, eh?' said the Inspector. 'That would be a 647 for us. A tourist's special.'

Kilmore took this to mean that 647 was a special health report code number. There was no reason he should have had even the slightest suspicion that the man he had in tow was Dick Minehead, an inspector at the local bus garage. He had been ordered to go to the hospital by his wife, who thought a little psychiatric help was called for, although he felt perfectly sound in mind and body.

They were joined in the reception area by Dr Tinkle.

'Ah, Dr Tinkle,' Kilmore said, 'I want you to meet the Inspector I've been telling you about. I'm just about to give him the guided tour. Would you care to join us?'

Tinkle and Minehead shook hands. 'Amazing, isn't it,' said the Inspector. 'You wait ages for a doctor and then two turn up at once.'

'Uh, quite,' said Tinkle. 'Now first of all we'd like to show you the kitchens. You'll find them so clean you could eat off the floor. If this were an hotel, we would rate five stars in the AA book.'

'Off you go then,' said the Inspector. 'Just the ticket. I'll follow behind.'

He gave a "ding-ding" sound. 'No standing inside, please. Hold on tight.'

As Tinkle and Kilmore, with the Inspector motoring along three strides behind them, moved down the corridor towards the kitchens they gave each other side-on looks. Matilda had warned them that the Inspector was an oddball, but they did not realise that he would prove to be certifiable.

When they reached the kitchens, the Inspector looked in through the open door without entering. 'Yes, very nice,' he said. 'Much superior to the canteen at the depot. As you say, spotless. All right, next stop. Hold tight. Ding ding.'

The doctors then led him to the women's surgical ward which had been scrubbed until everything gleamed and which was festooned with flowers in readiness for his inspection.

'Ah, the scenic route,' said Minehead. 'Very nice.'

'There's not a soul anywhere who could criticise the

84

condition and appearance of any of our wards,' said Kilmore, who had himself helped clean and scrub the floor and had red grazed knees to prove it.

The Matron had caught him on his hands and knees scouring away with a scrubbing brush.

'And just what do you think you're doing, Dr Kilmore?' she had said. 'Is this penance for your recent behaviour?'

'Just doing my bit to help keep the hospital clean,' said Kilmore.

The Matron was, as usual, not pleased. 'It just so happens, in case it has escaped your notice, that we have cleaners to do that job,' she said. 'It's disgraceful that you are trying to take the work away from them. Just wait until Clarence hears about this. His union will come down on you like a ton of bricks.'

Nurse May had overheard, and as the Matron went off in a huff she knelt down alongside Kilmore and kissed him on the cheek. 'You don't want to take any notice of her, darling,' she said. 'She's just an old scrubber.'

As Minehead inspected the ward through his two-way vision, Kilmore was glad that he had taken so much trouble to get it in sparkling condition. It was fit for royalty, and there was not a health inspector in the world who could have found fault. But there was something not to the liking of the bus inspector.

Minehead pointed at the far end of the ward where a recent amputee was being given instructions by a physiotherapist on how to manoeuvre a battery-driven wheelchair.

'Now that's breaking every rule in the book,' he said.
'I shall be reporting you for allowing learner drivers in
the bus lane. I have complained about this to the
Council time and again. Wrecks the schedules, it does.
They should not be allowed on the public highways
until they have gained full control of their vehicles.'

While the Inspector appeared to be looking away
from them, Dr Tinkle mimed to Kilmore with a
screwing motion of his forefinger to the side of his
head.

'Saw that,' said Minehead. 'The beauty of having
sight like mine is that it's like having eyes in the back of
my head. I'll be reporting you to the Council for gross
insolence towards me. This is not the first time it's
happened either, not by a long chalk. Down at the
depot they're always sniggering behind my back. But I
see them, and I report them. That's my forte, that is.
Seeing things that happen behind my back and then
making reports.'

'But I was not making any assertions against you,'
Tinkle lied. 'I was signalling to Dr Kilmore that it was
time to take you for an inspection of the, uh, psychiatric
ward.'

Minehead suddenly started walking backwards out
of the surgical ward. 'Oh no you don't,' he said. 'I'm
reversing out of here. You can't fool me. I've been an
inspector too long for anybody to be able to pull the
wool over my eyes. I know that once you get me into
that psychiatric place you won't let me out again.'

Kilmore shrugged as he followed the back-pedalling
Inspector Minehead out into the corridor. 'We'll give it

a miss then if you're that concerned,' he said. 'Let's go to men's surgical instead.'

Minehead performed an elaborate three-point turn and then held out an arm as a stop signal, allowing the two doctors to get in front of him. 'I don't mind that being on our route,' he said. 'Hold on tight. No standing inside. Ding, ding.'

As the small convoy made its way towards men's surgical at the far end of the corridor, Kilmore and Tinkle were suddenly aware of a commotion outside the ward. They arrived to find their way into the ward blocked by a line of hospital workers led by Clarence, who was holding a placard that read OFFICIAL UNION PICKET LINE.

'That's just as far as you go, gentlemen,' Clarence announced. 'You cannot cross this picket line.'

The doctors, with the bus inspector in tow, came to an untidy halt.

Clarence went heavily into union speak. 'We are now exercising our negotiated rights to protest over your action what has caused a crisis of confidence within my membership of which I am the officially and democratically elected spokesperson,' he said without pausing for breath. 'I am awaiting further instructions from my superiors at Union house, and until then we are withdrawing our labour, excepting that is in the labour ward.'

'But we're doctors,' protested Tinkle.

'Exactly,' said Clarence, glaring at Kilmore. 'You're doctors. Not cleaners. You're on the medical staff, *not* the cleaning staff. The only place you should clean and scrub is in the operating theatre.'

'But I was only trying to help,' said Kilmore.

Mrs Wilton was in the picket line. "elp?' she said. "elp? Is that what you call trying to put me out of a job? What right have you got to use a scrubbing brush and carbolic soap? 'Ow would you like it if I suddenly started looking down tonsils and removing warts? I've risked 'ousemaid's knee for this 'ospital, only to find that I'm in danger of being put out of work by a doctor who's never as much as cleaned a doorstep in his life. I'm disgusted with you, doctor. I never thought you'd stoop so low.'

'But I can explain,' said Kilmore. 'I needed to get the ward ready for an inspection.'

An impatient Inspector Minehead suddenly pushed his way to the front. 'Hello, a roadblock eh?' he said coming face to face with Clarence. 'I'll soon clear this little lot.'

'And who might you be?' Clarence said, trying hard to look him straight in the eyes but then settling for his nose.

'You know full well who I am,' said Minehead.

'Yes, I know you're an inspector,' said Clarence, who had often seen him supervising the buses in the high street. 'But that don't give you the right to come in here causing disruption to our picket line.'

'I'll have you know,' said Minehead, now nose to nose with Clarence, 'that I've crossed more picket lines than you've had cold dinners.'

'Don't you mean hot dinners?' said Clarence.

'No, they're never hot in our canteen. Now I demand that you re-open this route so that the doctors can

88

continue to give me a tour of inspection.'

Clarence placed his placard directly in front of Minehead, who looked either side of it. 'See this, comrade?' the hospital porter said. 'It says official, I repeat, official picket line. You will be risking serious consequences if you dare cross it. I have the power to close every hospital in the country, and – because of your uninvited interference – I'd get my brothers at the Transport and Workers' Union behind me to also close down every bus depot as well.'

Minehead suddenly reversed, and summoned Tinkle and Kilmore to follow him. They retreated back to halfway down the corridor, and the pickets cheered as the three of them withdrew.

'This is much more serious than I at first thought,' said the Inspector. 'Can you imagine how calamitous it would be if they closed down all the bus depots? It would throw the schedules into chaos. I don't like giving in to mob rule, but on this occasion I think it would be wisest to bypass the men's surgical ward. We must organise a detour, giving the main route a miss.'

'That's fine by us,' said Kilmore. 'But don't forget to include in your report that the ward was just as spotless as in women's surgical. I can assure you that it has been scrubbed cleaner than clean. In fact I think I might have given myself housemaid's knee doing it.'

'Don't worry, young man,' said Minehead. 'You can count on me to give a glowing report. Everything here is much, much better than I expected. When I left home this morning I dreaded coming in, but you've made me so welcome that I will report to everybody what a wonderful place this is, even for somebody like me who is perfectly sound in mind and body.'

'So where would you like us to make our next stop?' Tinkle asked.

'Oh, so it's a request stop, eh?' said the Inspector. 'Great. Well how about letting me see your garage?'

The two doctors glanced at each other and a hint of a satisfied smile passed between them. They were secretly delighted. This was going to have been the last call on their tour of inspection, and they were well prepared with a plan of action.

Minehead put out an arm to signal that he was moving off. 'Hold on tight,' he called. 'No standing inside. Garage next stop. Ding, ding.'

The pickets cheered and jeered as they watched the convoy steer a course for the exit, the doctors leading the way.

'This is only a battle victory,' announced Clarence. 'The war continues. Those doctors are up to something. They try to pretend they are just like us, but they are really a part of the ruling class. We must watch them very carefully.'

'Yes,' said the mortuary attendant 'particularly that Dr Kilmore. He's a weird one that one. Likes to pee over dead bodies.'

'How disgusting,' said Mrs Wilton. 'No wonder he needs a scrubbing brush and carbolic soap.'

There were two ambulances parked in the garage at the rear of the hospital, and room for one more which was out on an emergency call.

The Inspector was not at all impressed. 'Call this a garage?' he said, staring around like an architect on a planning mission. 'You couldn't squeeze one double decker in here. In fact, you couldn't even fit more than a couple of singles in. What a bloody disgrace. Wait until I report back on this to headquarters. I'll have this place closed down quicker than you can say ring the bell. Ding, ding.'

At a signal from Kilmore, the two doctors rushed at the Inspector. He made no attempt to resist as they grabbed him and bundled him into the back of one of the ambulances.

'My wife warned me this would happen,' said the Inspector as Kilmore fastened him flat down on the single, blanket-covered bed with the straps provided for dangerous patients.

Tinkle produced a Grundig tape-recorder from beneath the bed and pushed the "record" button.

'Right, Dick,' said Kilmore, sounding as menacing as possible, 'we know all about you.'

'So you know my name?' Dick Minehead said.

'We know *everything* about you.'

The Inspector shook his head in a resigned manner. 'I guessed as much,' he said to Kilmore, his wonky eyes trained on Tinkle. 'I suppose you've been speaking to my wife. Knew I should never have trusted her. My fault for marrying a conductress. Worst day's work of my life. I got a one-way ticket to hell.'

'We know all about the Mayor,' said Tinkle, suddenly and dramatically.

'So the mare's told you everything,' the Inspector said

91

sadly. 'Should have known it would happen one day. You obviously know all about the false reports that I was submitting to the Council?'

Kilmore and Tinkle nodded.

'It was my fault the Loxton depot was closed down,' he confessed, tears welling in his eyes. 'Falsified the reports. Said that the 97 was always running late. Didn't know the Council would use it as an excuse to shut the depot down. That greedy, bloody Mayor and his cohorts wanted the site for a building development. Just thought there'd be a warning, and that they'd kick out the driver But because of my reports they closed down the depot. How would you like to have that on your conscience?'

'But the Mayor told you to do it,' said Tinkle.

'True, but that's no excuse. The mare wanted revenge because that was the depot where all the trouble had been.'

'What trouble?' asked Kilmore.

'That was where the silly mare got involved in a row over fiddled fares.'

'The Mayor was fiddling the fares?' Tinkle said.

The Inspector nodded. 'Split the profits with the bus driver,' he said. 'Then I found out that the wicked mare and the driver had been having an affair.'

'The Mayor and the driver were having an affair?' Kilmore and Tinkle chorused.

The Inspector nodded as tears started to roll diagonally down his cheeks.

'This driver,' said Kilmore, 'it was a, um, a male driver?'

'Of course it bloody well was,' said the Inspector, looking at Kilmore and Tinkle at the same time as if they were mad. 'The mare is a horror at times, but has never been involved in anything kinky.'

He started to cry. 'I thought the mare loved me,' he said between sobs. 'But all the time it was the bus driver who was getting all the affection, and a share of the fare money.'

'So you and the Mayor had been lovers?' Kilmore found himself saying.

'Well of course we bloody had,' Minehead said. 'Twelve years we've been together. Nobody knew about it because we had to keep it from the Council, otherwise they'd have kicked us both out. The Council doesn't like employees having affairs.'

Kilmore and Tinkle exchanged glances with their eyebrows raised.

'Right, Inspector,' said Kilmore with as grave a voice as possible. 'Now that we know all about you and the Mayor, what are you going to do about the report on this hospital?'

'Well, I've got to be brutally honest about the garage,' he said. 'My report will have to recommend that it needs knocking down and a new one built in its place. Nice and large and airy, one in which you can get at least a dozen double deckers. Buses are no different to human beings, you know. They need room to breathe and to have their own space. The garage here is far too claustrophobic.'

'Yes, but what about the hospital itself?' said Kilmore.

'Can't see anything wrong with the place,' said the Inspector. 'Mind you, I'd like to see all of the wards without interference from those union wallahs. How about letting me continue the inspection tour now? No standing inside, please. Hold tight. Ding, ding.'

The two doctors left the ambulance for a hurried conference.

Kilmore whistled. 'God, have we got the Mayor by the balls and chain,' he said. 'The way Matilda had described him I thought he was a real old ram. Turns out he's a raving shirtlifter.'

'What are we going to do with the Inspector?' Tinkle said. 'You don't exactly have to have a degree in psychiatry to know the man is several sandwiches short of a picnic.'

'Bernie Biddle is due to report for his nightshift soon. We'll get him to run the inspector home in the ambulance, and then we can call off the watch. We've got our man, and we've got the Mayor. Once he hears what we've got over him on this tape he won't dare close down the hospital.'

They were just about to climb back into the ambulance when the garage door was pulled open. Bernie Biddle came in accompanied by a tall, skinny man with crossed eyes.

'Ah, doctors,' he said, 'look who I found snooping around the kitchens. It's the 'ealth and safety inspector, Percy Dick. He's 'ere for the Dick inspection.'

Kenneth Tinkle looked at Biddle, then at Dick and hoped desperately that it was a joke. 'Oooh, stop messing about,' he said.

As it dawned on him that Biddle was telling the truth, he sucked in his cheeks. 'Oh my giddy aunt,' he exclaimed, 'we've got the wrong Dick, Doc.'

8

HEALTH AND SAFETY INSPECTOR Percy Dick was lying strapped to the single bed in the second ambulance. Dr Kilmore and Dr Tinkle were preparing to give him the third degree treatment while Bernie Biddle sat in the other ambulance listening to Dick Minehead's carefully considered plans for the re-structuring of the transport system.

Tinkle switched on the Grundig tape-recorder, still shaking his head in stunned disbelief over the mix-up with the lookalike bus inspector. Both he and Kilmore believed it could yet work in their favour because he had made some startling revelations about Mayor Cocklewell.

Dick was nothing like as co-operative as the busman. They needed the robust Biddle to help them as they bundled him into the ambulance. 'I shall have your testicles on toast for this, Kilmore,' Dick had roared, looking at Tinkle. 'I've got friends in high places, men of real power who will make you all suffer.'

'The worse suffering,' said Kilmore, 'will come for those who abuse their power. People such as the Mayor and people such as *you*, Health Inspector Dickhead. We want a confession out of you before you will be allowed to leave this ambulance.'

'You can't link me with anything the Mayor may or may not have done,' said Dick, spitting defiance. 'As for keeping me a prisoner here, let me tell you that my office have instructions to send the police to look for me if I don't make contact within two hours. I always take that insurance when I go on a job. You've got nothing on me,'

'Give him a blanket,' said Tinkle.

Kilmore looked through the notes that had been supplied by Matilda. 'For a start, Mr Clever Dick, what about the closing down of the Ritz cinema?'

'The place was alive with fleas,' said Dick.

'Yes, fleas planted by you.'

'Prove it.'

'We have a transcript of a conversation you had with the Mayor in which you admitted it,' said Kilmore.

Dick's eyes momentarily became uncrossed as the shock hit him. 'It's that Matilda woman, isn't it?' he said. 'I knew she was trouble the minute I clapped eyes on her. The bitch.'

'Watch your tongue, you... you rogue,' said Tinkle in as threatening a tone as he could manage. 'You speak of the woman I love. At least, I think I love her. To be honest, I'm not ready for a firm commitment just at this moment, but it's certainly not a surface relationship and cannot be dismissed lightly as just another fling. I think we could eventually... '

'Yes, all right Kenneth,' said Kilmore. 'We'll save the agony aunt hour for later. Now listen to me Dick. We're not the slightest bit interested in what you've been up to during your rotten life. All we're interested in is saving our hospital from closure.'

'You haven't got a chance,' Dick said. 'The Mayor won't let anybody get in the way of him and his plan to

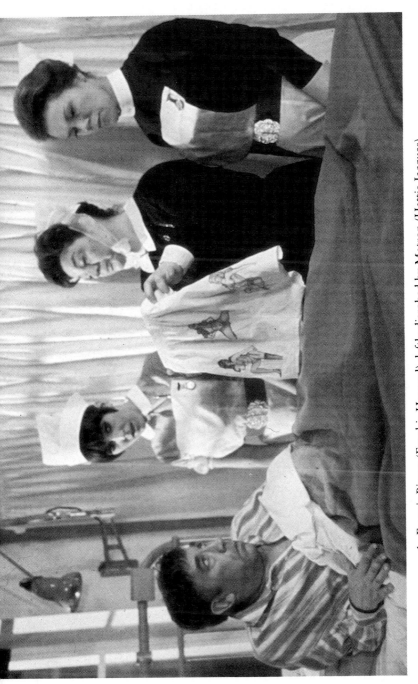

1. Francis Bigger (Frankie Howerd) deftly disrobed by Matron (Hattie Jacques).

2. Dr Tinkle (Kenneth Williams) takes charge of the more serious casualties. *BFI Stills*

3. Chloe Gibson (Joan Sims) exhibited as 'living' testimonial to the healing powers of Francis Bigger (Frankie Howerd). *BFI Stills*

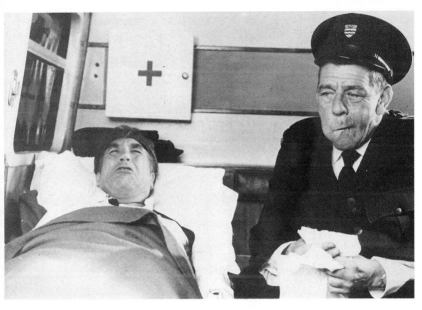

4. Ambulance attendant Sam (Harry Locke) shows little compassion towards patient Francis Bigger (Frankie Howerd). *BFI Stills*

5. Matron (Hattie Jacques) finds herself on the receiving end of a retaliatory blanket bath.

6. Dr Kilmore (Jim Dale) finds himself in an embarrassing situation after discovering that the 'suicide bid' of Nurse May

7. Dr Tinkle (Kenneth Williams) receives an unexpected night call from Matron (Hattie Jacques). *BFI Stills*

8. Francis Bigger (Frankie Howerd) questions Matron's bedside manner.

9. Gerald Thomas and Peter Rogers during
the shooting of *Carry On Doctor*. *BFI Stills*

10. The female patients revolt against Sister Hoggett (June Jago). *BFI Stills*

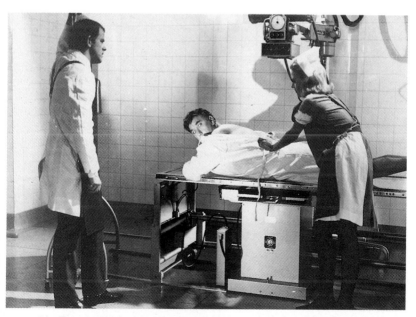

11. Francis Bigger (Frankie Howerd), in the hands of Nurse Parkin (Valerie van Ost). *BFI Stills*

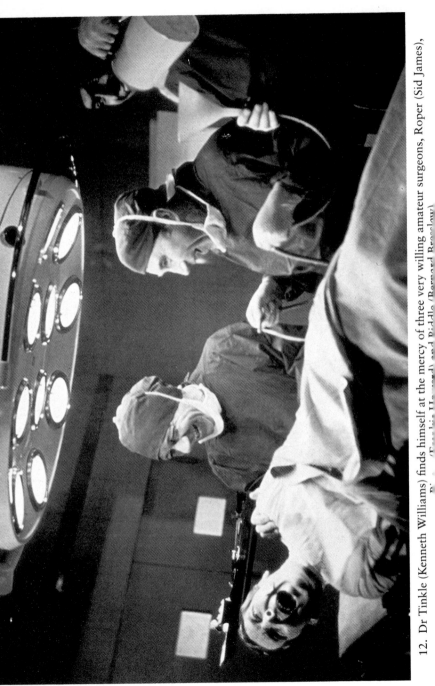

12. Dr Tinkle (Kenneth Williams) finds himself at the mercy of three very willing amateur surgeons, Roper (Sid James), (Frankie Howerd) and Biddle (Bernard Bresslaw)

knock down the hospital and to build a supermarket in its place. He stands to make a fortune out of it.'

'But what about all we've got on him?'

'What, for instance?'

'Well, about his affair with a local bus driver for starters. How would he like that splashed in the newspapers? Then there's his twelve-year love affair with the bus depot inspector. The man is obviously a serial bottom bandit.'

Dick showed off his tobacco-stained teeth as he laughed out loud.

'This *is* Mayor William Cocklewell we're talking about?' he said. 'You've got your lines as crossed as my eyes. The man is a notorious womaniser. He'll go for anything in a skirt. And I do mean *anything*. If it's female he fancies it. Ask Mata Hari Matilda. She should know.'

Tinkle grabbed hold of Dick by his collar, looked into his right eye and then his left and pulled a menacing face. 'Matilda has never allowed him to lay a hand on her,' he growled. 'And don't you suggest otherwise. You make me sick, Dick.'

'All I'm telling you,' Dick said, slowly and deliberately, 'is that you'll be laughed out of court if you try to prove that Mayor Cocklewell is anything but sexually straight. Admittedly it's the only part of his life that is straight.'

It at last dawned on both Kilmore and Tinkle that they could not rely on anything that had been told them by the bus inspector. The man was obviously off his trolley bus.

'Okay,' Kilmore said, 'so we cannot prove anything against the Mayor on the grounds of being a shirtlifter, but we have you on tape admitting that the Mayor stands to make a fortune out of getting the hospital knocked down so that a supermarket can be built in its place.'

Dick shook his head. 'You know and I know that tape recordings will not be accepted in a British court of law,' he said, with an arrogance born of a man who knows he has got his accusers on the run. ' All I'd have to say is that you tampered with the tape. Sorry, doctors, but you are proving yourselves to be bungling amateurs at the ducking-and-diving business. You should leave it to us pros.'

Kilmore signalled Tinkle to join him outside the ambulance.

'He's a hard case,' he said. 'I don't think we're going to be able to shake him into making a confession by just sitting there asking him questions. He ties us up every time.'

'Do you think he means it about the police being called if he doesn't make contact with his office, or is that just bluff?' Tinkle asked.

Kilmore scratched his head. 'We can't take any chances, and will just have to accept that he is telling the truth,' he said, 'This means we have got to move quickly. I think it's time for the special Nurse May treatment.'

Tinkle shuddered. 'Yes, I suppose it's our only alternative. You had better telephone her and tell her to get over here as quickly as possible.'

Kilmore went to the telephone. Tinkle returned to the ambulance to sit alongside the captive health inspector. Bernie Biddle sat listening to the rambling thoughts of Dick Minehead, who was telling him in detail how the bus service could be improved by allowing the drivers to mount pavements during the rush hour.

Ninety minutes had gone and there was no sign of Nurse May. Kilmore and Tinkle were getting increasingly anxious when there was a loud banging on the double doors of the garage. 'Open up in the name of the law,' came the shouted order in the unmistakeable tones of PC Shufflebottom.

Kilmore reluctantly pulled the doors open to discover the mountainous figure of the police constable looking down at him.

'Hello, hello, hello, what's going on here then?' asked the constable in his well-practised style. 'What are *you* doing in here?'

'Well I am a doctor and this *is* a hospital,' said Kilmore.

Tinkle came out of the ambulance to see what was happening.

'You here as well?' said Shufflebottom. 'I might have guessed it. You still can't be consenting hadults in a hambulance. That is a means of public transport for people what is hill.'

'Don't be a clot, Stinker,' said Kilmore. 'We're here on hospital business.'

'Well maybe you can help me in my inquiries,' the constable said. 'I'm looking for an inspector what is meant to have been here at the hospital. He has not contacted his office and I have been sent to find him.'

'Have you got a description?' asked Kilmore.

'Tall, thin chap,' said Shufflebottom.

'Any distinguishing features?'

'Apparently he has one eye what looks at the other.'

'Ah, *that* inspector,' said Kilmore. 'It just so happens that I can take you right to him.'

He turned and led the constable towards the first ambulance where Dick Minehead was sending Biddle almost into a coma with a discourse on how they should introduce triple-decker buses, with exits from the roof so that passengers could enter their offices through first-floor windows.

Biddle had undone the straps that were fastening Minehead to the bed in the hope that he would escape and stop giving him GBH to the earholes. But he was perfectly happy to lie back talking to his captive audience about his vision for the future of the bus service.

Shufflebottom jackknifed and hauled his huge body into the back of the ambulance. He looked down at Dick. 'Are you the Inspector Dick what has been touring the hospital today?' he asked, convinced he had found his man when Minehead looked wide of his crouching six foot five inch frame (or seven foot three inches if you include his helmet) and nodded.

'I am he, but I'd appreciate less familiarity,' said Minehead. 'Plain Inspector will suffice. What do you want with me?'

'Your office was concerned about you,' said

Shufflebottom. 'They wondered why you hadn't rung in to tell them where you are.'

'I've been kept too busy here at the hospital,' the Inspector said. 'These gentlemen have been kind enough to take me on the tourist's route, and they have been noting down my plans to unclog our roads.'

Shufflebottom suddenly looked closely at Bernie Biddle. 'I thought hearses not hambulances were what you usually travel in,' he said.

'Yes, guv,' said Biddle, 'that is usually the case, but there's a shortage of ambulance drivers because of a lightning strike and so I've called in to offer my services, kind of thing like. Can't have the ambulances off the road, can we?'

'Or the buses,' said Minehead, who was staring at the front of the ambulance making a close study of Shufflebottom at the back. 'Aren't you the constable who directs traffic at the high street crossroads?'

Shufflebottom puffed out his chest and tried to stand erect, thumping his helmet against the roof of the ambulance. 'That is me what directs the high street traffic,' he said, with the sort of pride you would expect from a craftsman discussing his work.

'Well you should be ashamed of yourself,' Minehead said, with real vehemence in his voice.

Shufflebottom blinked like a boxer taking a punch on the nose.

'You were continually giving the bus drivers wrong signals,' he added, getting to his feet and waving his arms around.

'This,' he said twirling his right arm, 'signifies right

101

of way for traffic coming from the right. Right?'

'No, left,' said Shufflebottom, confused by the way Minehead was looking left and right at the same time.

'Can't you see straight, sonny?' Minehead said, now twirling his left arm. 'This means right of way for traffic coming from the left. Right?'

The constable had lost all sense of direction. 'You're talking like a bus inspector,' he said.

Kilmore, Tinkle and Biddle all tensed. 'I *am* a bus inspector,' said Minehead.

'But I thought you were a health and safety inspector,' said Shufflebottom, his suspicions beginning to rise like antennas.

' Well I'm here to have my health inspected and I am always interested in safety,' he said to the background sound of sighs of relief from the two doctors and Biddle. 'And talking of safety, I am going to submit a report on you, young man, to see to it that you are banished for ever from directing traffic.'

Before the mortally embarrassed Shufflebottom could respond there was a rat-a-tat knocking on the garage door. As the constable was blocking the way out of the ambulance, he clumsily got out and slid the garage doors open. His embarrassment factor was doubled when he found himself looking down into the considerable frontage of Nurse May. In her hands she had a bowl of steaming soapy water, and over her arm hung a long rubber tube with a small funnel on the end of it.

'Sorry I'm late, darlings,' she said. 'Got held up by a bleedin' picket line. Now where's the victim? Whose

102

bottom has this got to go up?'

Shufflebottom's lips moved but no sound came out. Kilmore and Tinkle were now at his side.

Nurse May looked at Minehead, who was peering out of the back of the ambulance, his gaze seeming to be fixed on the far corner of the wall.

''ere. That ain't old what's it,' she said. 'You know, thingumebob. The bloke from...'

'Ah, thank you, Nurse May,' said Kilmore, deliberately interrupting as he took the bowl of water and the tube from her. 'We can now get the grease stain off the bottom of my trousers. And as for old what's it, he's been taken for a ride.'

Shufflebottom stood watching, his antennas rising again.

'You can help, constable,' Kilmore said, pushing the bowl into his hands. 'Right, Tinkle, I'll bend over and then you pour the water into the tube funnel and make sure it goes on to the seat of my trousers.'

The constable handed the bowl to Nurse May. 'Here, miss, you take this,' he said, 'I've got better things to do than get involved in this sort of malarkey. This just might come under the heading of consenting adults, and I cannot be seen to be an accessory. A man bending over in front of another may constitute an offence, even if he keeps his trousers on. I must look up the law book when I return to the station and get to the bottom of it.'

'So what are you going to do now, officer?' said Tinkle.

'I'm going to escort the inspector back to his office,' Shufflebottom said.

'Uh, I've got a better idea,' said Kilmore. 'Bernie here can run the inspector home in the ambulance, and then drop you back at the station.'

'I can?' said Bernie. 'I mean I can. 'Course I can. Climb aboard, Constable. This shouldn't take long, not with your sense of direction.'

As Bernie started up the engine, Kilmore and Tinkle stifled a laugh when they heard Minehead calling out at the back.

'Hold tight,' he shouted. 'No standing inside please. Ding, ding.'

Percy Dick had been turned over on his face, and the straps holding him to the single bed in the ambulance tightened.

'We are going to have to take drastic measures, Inspector, to try to make you co-operate with us,' Kilmore said threateningly.

'There's nothing that will make me grass on the Mayor,' he said, 'mainly because by fingering him I would be incriminating myself.'

'Well we're not going to finger you, Mr Bloody Health and Safety,' said Tinkle. 'We're going to *tube* you. In other words, up yours!'

'Nurse May,' said Kilmore, 'his trousers please.'

There was not a nurse in the universe who could match the speed of Nurse May in bringing down a pair of man's trousers. Inspector Dick's trousers were down below his knees in a twinkling of an eye. His grey Y-fronts quickly followed.

'What the f---,' Dick started to say, his bare bottom

now exposed to the unimpressed gaze of Nurse May, Kilmore and Tinkle, who had all seen such a sight hundreds of times before. The difference was they were usually working on reasonably willing patients.

'Nurse, the tube,' said Kilmore.

Nurse May handed him the tube. 'Right, Inspector, you've got five seconds to decide whether you are going to help us in the battle to save our hospital,' Kilmore said. 'If you don't respond this tube will be shoved into an unspeakable place while we give you what is known in the trade as the bowel bomb.'

'In other words an enema,' said Tinkle. 'And with enemas like this, who needs friends?'

The suddenly petrified Dick would have sent the Mayor to the bloody Tower rather than have the tube treatment, but he had fainted at the mere prospect of what the doctors said was about to happen. Kilmore took his silence to mean stubborn resistance, and – with the thought of a closed-down hospital as his driving force – he pushed the tube roughly into the inspector's rectum.

Tinkle poured the warm soapy water into the funnel, and Nurse May concentrated on clearing up the resultant wastage.

The messy, painful performance was all over in less than five minutes, but it was several more minutes before Dick came round.

'What have you done to me?' he screamed, tears running straight rather than diagonally down his face. 'I'll never be the same man again.'

The doctors unstrapped him, and as the Inspector sat

up they saw the effect the shock of the enema had had on him. His eyes had straightened.

Dick held his hands in front of his face, and then moved them left and right as he followed them with both eyes at once. Left, right and then straight ahead. He held his head perfectly still, and then moved his eyes from side to side like a man in the Centre Court audience at Wimbledon. The Inspector looked up and then he looked down, his eyes working in tandem. He tried looking at Dr Kilmore by tilting his head to his customary forty-five degrees and looking in the direction of the ambulance door. All he could see was the ambulance door. Then he looked directly at the doctor, and saw the doctor. He could not believe what he was seeing.

Nurse May and the two doctors watched him as if he were a new-born child. Tinkle shook his head. 'The miracles of medical science,' he said.

'Unbelievable,' said Kilmore. 'We have cured him of the worst case of squintitis I have ever seen.'

Fear had gripped Dick. 'How can I face the world looking like this?' he said between sobs. 'How can I do my job without being able to see round corners any more?'

'There, there, darling,' said Nurse May. ' You look really 'andsome now.'

They were words that had never before been uttered to Dick. He was more accustomed to being called a boss-eyed or cross-eyed git. Children in the street used to taunt him and shout, 'Eye, eye, that's yer lot.'

He looked straight at Nurse May. 'You're not just

saying it, are you?' he said.

'No, 'course not. Frank Sinatra would like eyes like yours. Here, have a butcher's in this mirror.'

Dick looked straight ahead into the ambulance mirror that faced him. It was the first time he had ever been able to look himself straight in the eyes.

He started to cry again, this time with unbridled happiness. 'I don't know how to thank you, doctors,' he said. 'You've given me a whole new outlook on life.'

'There's an easy way to thank us,' said Kilmore. 'Just give the hospital the inspection report that it deserves. You know this place should not be closed down. Now you have first-hand or even first-look experience of what wonders we can perform here.'

'I'll do that for you, no problem,' Dick said. 'But I'll tell you now, it won't make the slightest bit of difference with the Mayor. He is going to shut this hospital down no matter what. All I can promise is that I will do my best to stop him by writing such a glowing report that those Council members he's not got in his pocket will vote to block any proposal to close the Haven.'

Kilmore and Tinkle shook him warmly by the hand. Nurse May kissed him on either cheek, and he managed to keep his eyes in check as he stole a glance at her appealing appendages. His eyes came through this observation test unmoved.

The doctors had to assist Dick as he left the ambulance and walked out of the garage. For the first few steps he struggled to keep a straight line, and he found he had to blink several times in the gathering evening gloom before he was able to focus properly.

'You'll soon get used to your new, unimpaired vision,' said Kilmore. 'Just take it easy for a couple of days, and then you can look forward to enjoying your new life and you will never be cross again.'

It was a smiling Dick who walked – even though he felt like dancing – through the hospital gates. He was still a little unsteady but just about the happiest he had been in his life.

He turned and waved to Kilmore, Tinkle and Nurse May. They walked back into the hospital together with a spring in their step, warmed by the glow of satisfaction that made their jobs so worthwhile.

Had they looked back, they would have seen Dick step off the pavement directly into the path of a double decker bus driven by the mad Inspector Minehead.

As the health and safety inspector lay beneath the wheels, a thoughtful passer-by covered his eyes with two coins.

Dick would have enjoyed reading the coroner's report that stated: 'This was a man with apparently perfect vision, and bowels that were in pristine condition.'

9

RELUCTANTLY, Dr Kilmore decided he had to share the secret of the Mayor's closure plan with Clarence which would inevitably lead to the dreaded Matron being kept abreast (the operative word) of events. It was the only way he could think of breaking the union strike that was threatening to paralyse the running of the hospital without any help from the Mayor.

The fact that the wretched Dick had not, to the best of his knowledge, been able to submit a favourable report before his untimely demise meant that they were back to square one in the battle to save the hospital.

When he first approached Clarence for peace talks, the union leader refused to speak to him. 'We have sent Dr Kilmore to Coventry,' he told the go-between Nurse May.

'Well he ain't gone,' said the nurse. 'He's upstairs in the staff room waiting to talk to you.'

'Sorry, Nurse May, but he has become *persona non grata.*'

'No, he's still the same Jimmy Kilmore,' she said. 'He's told me that he wants to tell you something extremely important that will affect everybody's future. Yours, mine, everybody's. He says he has only the interests of the hospital at heart, and that he must be allowed to communicate with you.'

'Well he'll have to go through the proper union

channels,' Clarence said. 'I would be breaking union rules if I, in my trusted position as father of the chapel, exchanged words with him. He will have to approach me by speaking to the branch secretary.'

'Who's that?' asked Nurse May.

'Me,' said Clarence.

'But he can't speak to you,' she said.

'That is quite correct.'

'Then how on earth does he tell you what he needs to tell you?'

'That is for him to worry about, not me. It was him who thoughtlessly started all this by doing the cleaning work that is rightly the work of the people whose job it is to do the cleaning work.'

Nurse May frowned as she tried to follow what Clarence was saying. 'But he was only trying to save the hospital,' she said.

'Save it?' said Clarence. 'Oh no, miss. He was trying to *clean* it. On his knees he was, with a scrubbing brush and a bar of Lifebuoy. It was our Matron who caught him red-handed.'

'But I'm telling you, Clarence, that he was only doing it to stop the Mayor from closing down the hospital.'

Nurse May had unknowingly found the red rag to the bull that was buried deep inside Clarence. 'The Mayor?' he said, his eyes suddenly bulging. 'Mayor bloody Cocklewell? What's that repulsive, reptile of a man up to now? What's he got his thieving, money-grabbing fingers into?'

'That's exactly what Dr Kilmore wants to talk to you about,' said Nurse May, jumping up and down in a mixture of aggravation and excitement.

Clarence suddenly abandoned his stubborn stance. 'In that case,' he announced, 'I will now this instant convene an extraordinary meeting with the union secretary by the powers invested in me as the father of the chapel to get a temporary lifting of the order preventing me from conversing with the doctor. Excuse me one moment, please, Nurse.'

Clarence went into what seemed an almost hypnotic trance for twenty seconds. Nurse May was just about to feel his pulse when he snapped out of it.

'Right,' he said. 'I've just held a meeting, and it has been unanimously agreed that I can talk to the doctor but only on the understanding that I can immediately send him back to Coventry should I feel it right and proper to do so.'

Nurse May nodded. 'All right, darling,' she said. 'While you're up in the staff room talking to him I'll look up the train times.'

Dr Kilmore and Dr Tinkle welcomed Clarence to the staff room like an old friend. 'I'm so glad you've had the good sense to drop this Coventry nonsense and have come to see us,' Kilmore said. 'I promise you that you have made a wise and right decision that will be for the good of the hospital, which is something I know we both have at heart.'

'That's as maybe,' said Clarence, 'But I have to warn you, sir, that this may be only a temporary respite from the union action that has been taken against you. I am duty bound to tell you that you have caused untold

111

anxiety and fretting among my union members in this hospital by carrying out duties what is exclusively the responsibility of them what is responsible for the said duties.'

'Quite,' said Kilmore. 'But I promise I meant no harm. There were reasons, good reasons, why we could not divulge exactly why we wanted the wards looking cleaner than ever.'

'They'd better be good ones, sir. Otherwise my union members will be taking *you* to the cleaners.'

Over the following fifteen minutes Kilmore and Tinkle gave Clarence full chapter-and-verse of the Mayor's evil plan to demolish Haven Hospital and how he intended to build a supermarket in its place. They explained about the planned tour of inspection by Percy Dick, the late health and safety inspector, only omitting the embarrassing chapter about the quite understandable identity mix-up.

At every mention of Mayor Cocklewell Clarence turned purple, and appeared to be giving an impression of a bulldog eating a thistle.

When all had been laid on the table, Clarence stood up from the sofa and went into his twenty second trance. Kilmore and Tinkle were just about to consider if a kiss of life was necessary when he snapped out of it and addressed the two doctors as if at a union delegation meeting.

'First of all, brothers,' he said, 'it is encumbered upon me to inform you that I have just had a meeting with a fellow union executive and the outcome is that I would like to say how sorry I am that we misinterpreted and misunderstood what were your good intentions in scrubbing the ward floors.

'In the given circumstances and knowing what you knew then and what I know now it was perfectly understandable and acceptable what you did, and on behalf of my fellow union delegates I officially withdraw the send-to-Coventry motion and humbly apologise for any embarrassment what has been caused.'

Kilmore and Tinkle indicated their acceptance of his apology and took a breath for him.

'I have had personal experience of the depths to which the said Mayor Cocklewell will sink for his own ends,' he continued. 'We have had several run-ins, the worst of which was when he had the bowling green where I spend my few relaxing moments ripped up so that he could turn it into a car park from which I know he has a rake-off. Then there was the time when he put those horrible new parking meter things right outside the hospital, and I have it on good authority, although I cannot prove it and I wish that I could, that he personally pocketed the fines that had to be paid by the ambulance drivers what I represent in my capacity as a union organiser and negotiator.'

Clarence started to choke on his words when he came to what was now an obviously sensitive issue. 'On a completely private note just between you two good gentlemen doctors and me, I have deeply personal and private reasons for wanting to chop the Mayor's balls off, pardon my French,' he said haltingly, with tears welling in his eyes. 'It is no secret here in the hospital

113

that the Matron and I have formed a close association that is so far purely platonic but, fingers crossed and God willing, with the distinct prospects of deeper involvement when Gertrude is finally free of that first worthless husband of hers.'

Kilmore and Tinkle were on the edge of their seats. That was two secrets to which they were privy. They did not know that the Matron had a husband in the closet, and they did not know that her name was Gertrude. What, they wondered, could be coming next?

'This Mayor Cocklewell,' said Clarence, spitting out the name, 'is the sewer rat who at a recent Town Hall reception propositioned the lady who has my heart. He plied her with medium sherry, sweet talked her into his chambers and then tried to have his way with her over the mayoral seat of office.'

Both Kilmore and Tinkle suddenly remembered the words of Inspector Dick: 'He will chase anything in a skirt... and I do mean anything.' With the image of the matron struggling on the mayoral seat flooding their minds, they looked at each other and said in unison: 'He really did mean *anything*.'

Clarence was too intent on unburdening himself to take any notice of their chorus. 'Matron had the presence of mind to knee him where it hurts,' he said proudly. 'But not before he had put his hand where no man's hand had been before.'

Kilmore and Tinkle each had the identical silent thought: 'So where did her husband used to put his hands?'

'The Mayor rubbed his hands on the Matron's

114

badge,' Clarence said. 'It caused her untold mental anguish. When she told me I wanted to go round to the Town Hall and give him a good thrashing, but Matron said there was no need. She had done the deed herself. That brave woman described to me how she stuck the mace inside his trousers and then fired him like a human arrow against the wall using those daft braces what he wears as a catapult. She made sure he would never make advances to her again.'

Kilmore and Tinker were speechless, but Clarence still had plenty to say for himself.

'In my honourable and distinguished role as representative of all the workers in this hospital – not including doctors and nurses, no offence – I must, of course, refrain from allowing any personal feelings of malice to cloud my judgement and I must be at all times even-handed. But if I get the chance, I will mutilate the Mayor. Yes, mutilate him. I already had reason to tear him apart with my bare hands, but now to find what he is planning to do to a hospital what serves the community is beyond all understanding of decent men and so far out of order as to be criminal. The man is a swine of the first order.'

Clarence sat down, and there was a moment's silence almost out of respect for his deep feelings.

It was Kilmore who broke the silence. 'We are enormously sympathetic about the position in which you find yourself, Clarence.'

'Thank you, sirs,' he said. 'You are gentlemen of the first order and I am mortified at what we made you go through over the cleaning business. There are not words in my uneducated head of sufficient weight to convey how distressed and sorry I am for the inconvenience and concern what we caused you. All I can ask is your forgiveness and understanding. We could only act on the facts as we knew them, and on this occasion we got it terribly, terribly wrong. I can only plead that you take the mitigating circumstances into account, and accept that we meant you no harm personally and that we were driven by the desire for what we saw at the time as fair play to our union brothers and sisters what are in the cleaning department.'

'That's all forgotten,' said Kilmore, embarrassed by the way Clarence was on his knees begging forgiveness. 'What we must do now is put all personal feelings and grievances to one side and concentrate on coming up with a plan to stop the Mayor closing us down. Have you got any ideas as to what combative action we can take, Clarence?'

That was the equivalent of asking Percy Thrower if he had any garden seeds. Clarence rose again from the sofa and started to pace the staff room like a caged tiger. Then he stood and went into one of his trances. As he snapped out of it, he staggered a little as if the mental power he had generated had been too much for his head to take.

'I've just had a union meeting at top executive level,' he said. 'What we have decided after due consideration of all the facts is that we must hit the Mayor and his partners in crime with a united front. We cannot stand alone and expect to beat a man what has powerful friends in his pocket. We are going to put all our union

116

muscle into this campaign, and beat him by people power. And *then* I'm going to knock the shyte out of him.'

Kilmore and Tinker wondered what sort of monster they had unleashed. They were just glad he was on their side.

At around about the same time that the doctors were forming their alliance with Clarence and his union executive, the Mayor was delivering a moving oratory at the monthly meeting of the Council.

'The late, great and much lamented Percival Dick,' he said, 'were a man of the greatest integrity, whose detailed reports on matters of 'ealth and safety were works of art. His imagination knew no bounds. He were a reet good 'un whose loyalty to me and t'Council were unswerving, except that time when he refused to recommend t'closing of t'Crown and Anchor pub because he 'ad lodgings there. That apart, in his time he 'elped close down more places in t'borough than any man alive... or deceased, for that matter.

'The fact that he never looked you straight in the eyes were neither here nor there as far as I were concerned. He 'ad his own way of looking at life, and I for one am glad that he, uh, double-crossed my path. We will never see his like again, not now that you can get squints straightened on t'National 'ealth. And talking of t'National 'ealth...'

The Mayor removed from his briefcase a one-page document, forged by his own fair hand. 'I 'ave here in my 'and a piece of paper,' he said, waving it above his head in the best Neville Chamberlain tradition. 'It bears

117

the signature of Herr, I mean Mr Percival Dick and is his very last report for the urgent attention of t'Council. This devastating document were found on his still-warm body as he lay under the bus that brought such a tragic and premature end to what were a wonderful and extremely productive life. I shall read it out for your ears only:

"'It is my sad and solemn duty to report that 'aven 'ospital 'as become a death trap that should be closed down before somebody dies there in a tragic accident caused by falling masonry, food poisoning, dysentery, rotting timber crashing on their 'ead, malaria, foot 'n' mouth disease, bubonic plague, rabies or some other form of illness brought on by the unhealthy condition of the place that I state, quite categorically and without prejudice, is unsafe for occupation. It is my expert and considered opinion, reached I must say independently and without anybody trying to tell me what to put in my report, that the 'ospital should not only be pulled down but that a building more in keeping with the environment of our town should be built in its place. Something like a supermarket, for instance, that would make life so much easier and more convenient for the women of the borough who have to traipse around the market stalls in all kinds of filthy weather doing their shopping. How much more sensible and convenient to have all the shopping under one roof, and wire prams on wheels to push your purchases around on. Surely this makes much more sense than an 'ospital which takes up valuable space and makes people iller instead of better. I am scribbling down this report just before I leave the 'ospital, just in case I get knocked down by a bus. It would be a terrible thing if I were to go without 'aving warned t'Council of the dangers lurking in the 'aven 'ospital. Signed just before I go through the 'ospital gates, Percival Dick, 'ealth and safety inspector."'

The Mayor paused, and with skilled timing slowly looked around at the Councillors, allowing the full impact of the dramatic statement to sink in.

'Now what could be a better memorial to a great servant of this borough than for us to grant his last wish?' the Mayor said with forced emotional choking on his words. 'Just dwell for a moment on his final words, written in his own hand in this damning report. He warned that the 'ospital had become a death trap and then just moments later he is tragically killed. Where? Right outside the death trap of the 'ospital that he had warned about, that's where. Now surely we as caring, conscientious Councillors should now be looking to honour our late and much mourned colleague in the way he would have most wanted. Let his lasting memorial be the demolition of 'aven 'ospital. We can put up a plaque in his memory and record, "This was the site of the 'aven 'ospital razed to the ground in loving memory of Pervical Dick R-I-P.'

There were murmurs of assent as the Mayor sat down, a large white handkerchief to his eyes.

The deputy treasurer, who just happened to be the Mayor's son-in-law, jumped to his feet in response to the white handkerchief signal: 'I move that the hospital be shut down. Right now. We cannot possibly go on risking the health of our townspeople.'

119

'Anybody care to second that?' asked the Mayor, looking directly at his golfing partner and the man he was proposing as next mayor, Harvey Bentt. He raised his hand as if it had been pulled by an invisible string. 'I'll second it,' he said. 'I know I speak for future generations when I say that it is best to do away with the hospital.'

He glanced down at the notes that the Mayor had given him. 'And while we're about it we should take this opportunity to fire a warning shot across the bows of the National Health, what is an unnecessary drain on our economy,' he read. 'What we need is an hospital, a privately run and relocated hospital, where we get better not worse.'

There was a rumble of agreement around the chamber. 'Reet,' said the Mayor, 'I'll put it to the vote. If, as I expect and demand, it is a "yes" vote, we will keep the news secret until tomorrow so that we can get it splashed in the *Mercury* and so make the biggest possible impact before the 'ospital can come back with some twaddle about them being unfairly or summarily treated. Those in favour of closing 'aven 'ospital what has become a death trap say aye.'

There was a loud chorus of "ayes", and it was noted for the record in memory of Percival Dick that not one of them was crossed.

It was a distressed Matilda who hurried to bring news of the Council decision to Kilmore in the casualty department. It was the last thing he wanted to hear at the end of a hard shift during which he had cut out a bunion, syringed ears, inspected some haemorrhoids, removed a cyst, stitched a gashed head, set two broken legs in plaster and had removed the inevitable bucket from an idiot's head. He also spent an hour trying to replace a severed hand, only to find it was a prank by medical students. The hand had been cut off a corpse, and the 'patient' brought into casualty had lost his hand in a childhood accident.

Kilmore sighed at the memory of his student days and the larks he himself had got up to, including once nailing the Matron's shoes to her bedroom floor. Such was the strength of the buffalo of a woman that she had torn up two floorboards and come on her round of the wards like a skier. She was never able to pin the prank on Kilmore, but she had her well-founded suspicions and had since taken every chance to get back at him.

Now they needed to work together against a common enemy, the Mayor and the Council.

It was well past midnight, and both Tinkle and Clarence were in their beds. They could be told the news in the morning, but Kilmore decided it was his duty to immediately inform the Matron of the Council vote for the closure of the hospital. He knew that she would still be up because she had made one of her dreaded snap ward inspections just ten minutes before Matilda had passed on the Council decision.

The night-shift cleaners were in, and one of them had left her bucket, scrubbing brush and soap in the corridor leading to the Matron's quarters while she went off for a well-earned cuppa. To keep the noise to

121

a minimum, Kilmore crept down the corridor and it was quite understandable that he did not expect to encounter a bar of soap on the floor as he concentrated on what he should say to the Matron.

It was while on tip toe that he trod on the soap. He performed a spectacular somersault that would have earned him high marks in the diving pool and managed somehow to come down with his head landing in the bucket. As he stood up looking like a knight preparing for battle the dirty water in the bucket poured over his shoulders and drenched his white doctor's coat. Now Kilmore knew exactly what was meant by the phrase, 'It's bucketing down'.

Good sense got the better of him, and he decided that now was not perhaps a good time to be having a quiet tête-à-tête with the Matron, and he considered that in the circumstances it was best to try to get as far away from her as possible. Blindly, he tried to set on a path back towards the casualty department but he was completely disoriented and was crashing from wall to wall of the corridor still en route for the Matron's quarters.

Kilmore could not see where he was going as he attempted to tug the bucket off his head, but he could hear perfectly. As he rattled and rolled along the walls, he heard a familiar voice. 'What on earth is that horrendous noise?' shouted the Matron. 'You'll wake up the entire hospital. Who's inside this bucket, for goodness sake? Come on, you can't disguise yourself. I'll soon find out who you are.'

Kilmore stopped struggling with the bucket, and

122

silently weighed up what the chances were of remaining anonymous.

He had his mind made up for him by the Matron. 'Speak up this instant,' she said, prodding him in the stomach with what he presumed was the cleaner's mop. 'I know you're one of our young doctors. Now own up before I call the night porter to have you evicted.'

'It's me, Dr Kilmore,' he confessed, his voice echoing around his head.

'I might have guessed it,' Matron said. 'What on earth are you doing with that bucket on your head and at this time in the morning? Drunk again, I suppose.'

'No, Matron. I took a trip.'

'Ah, drugs, eh? That's even more serious than drinking on duty. I've heard all about the trips you young people are on with the hallucinatory LSD. These so-called swinging sixties will be the death of us all, mark my words.'

She prodded him again with the mop. 'Well, for this, Dr Kilmore, I will see that you are not only suspended from hospital duty but also kicked out of the medical profession completely,' she said, managing to sound like a criminal court judge handing out a long sentence.

Kilmore felt familiar comforting arms around him. 'Don't worry, Matron,' he heard Nurse May say. 'I'll look after him. You go and get your beauty sleep.'

At this point, Kilmore could not hold back an explosion of laughter that could be heard rattling around the bucket.

'Come on, Jimmy,' said Nurse May, who had just come off duty. 'I'll guide you to casualty.'

The next thing Kilmore heard was the night doctor. 'Oh, here we go,' he said. 'The inevitable idiot with his head stuck in a bucket.'

'Just another night in the hectic life of Haven Hospital,' Kilmore thought to himself as he waited for the bucket to be prised off his head. 'But how many more nights are left?'

He decided he would wait until the morning before announcing the disturbing tidings from the Council.

Kilmore also decided that he would leave it to Clarence to tell the Matron. If he went to her with the news he was worried, and with some justification, that she would shoot the messenger.

10

TRUE TO HIS WORD, Clarence mobilised the full union force. Trains and buses stopped running, dustbins were left unemptied, lorries were not allowed to unload and, as his contribution, the hospital chaplain gave only half the sign of the cross. Pickets surrounded the Town Hall shouting, 'Mayor Cocklewell out... Save the hospital, knock down the Town Hall instead.'

That very thought had gone through the Mayor's mind years earlier, but he had been tipped off by a surveyor that there was such serious subsidence that only a single-storey building could be erected in its place, so any profit margins would be negligible.

The union action back-fired when the cunning Mayor carefully orchestrated a scare story in the newspapers which ran front page headlines such as REDS UNDER THE HOSPITAL BEDS and STRIKE HOSPITAL MATRON IS A MARXIST.

Cocklewell planted the Matron story when he found out that she had an account at Marks & Spencer, so he was only slightly bending the facts. He managed to convince reporters that the strikes were a Communist plot aimed at bringing down the government.

The one thing that Cocklewell had miscalculated was the fury his actions were to unleash in the Matron. He had already had experience of her counter-attacking strengths when he made the mistake of trying to grope her in the mayoral chambers, but that was nothing to what she was planning for him from the moment that

Clarence had revealed the closure plans. Her first reaction was to punch a fist down on her desk with such force that it went straight through to the drawer. After the hospital carpenter had been called to cut free her hand, she quietly plotted her personal plan of campaign. She elected to leave the men to waffle and talk around in circles while she took the direct route. Clarence could *talk* about knocking the shyte out of the Mayor. She would provide action to go with his words.

A long-winded union meeting was just about to start when the Matron, dressed in her ankle-length cape and wearing tight-fitting leather gloves, slipped out of the rear exit and made her way on foot the mile to the Town Hall. The picket line surrounding the Edwardian red brick building was no match for the Matron. The union official who misguidedly exercised his right to try to persuade her not to cross the line, not knowing to whom he was putting the argument for solidarity, was felled with a perfectly delivered, breathtaking right hook to the solar plexus.

The bemedalled, black uniformed commissionaire standing guard inside the oak-panelled double doors confronted the uninvited and unwelcome caller. He was an ex-soldier who had seen service at El Alamein and was as tough as old army boots, but a left to the ribs and a right uppercut to the chin quickly had him doubled over inspecting his laces. An alert receptionist, witnessing the angry arrival of this caped crusader whirlwinding through the foyer, ducked down behind the counter with a telephone receiver in her hand.

She dialled 999 as the Matron strode purposefully

towards the winding staircase leading to the first floor office of the Mayor. 'Help,' the breathless receptionist said in an urgent whisper. 'There's a mad woman loose in the Town Hall.'

The duty sergeant looked around to see who was available to investigate the incident. Everybody was tied up and so, reluctantly, he contacted the constable on traffic duty at the crossroads a minute from the Town Hall. It was PC Shufflebottom who was given the assignment.

The Matron had raced up the stairs three at a time. She knew exactly where the Mayor's office was situated, and she sensed, correctly, that he would be in there masterminding the closure campaign. Matilda met her as the outer door swung open. 'This is a pleasant surprise, Matron,' she said with a welcoming smile.

'Out of my way,' she snarled, pushing Matilda so hard that she bounced across her office and landed back in her chair. She then threw open the inner door to the Mayor's office, where her steely gaze fell on the petrified Cocklewell sheltering behind the Deputy Mayor, and his son-in-law. His fat jowls were shaking around the cigar clenched tightly between his teeth like white blancmange quivering around a chocolate cone.

Harvey Bentt, the man who would be Mayor, gulped at the sight of the Matron filling the doorway like a giant bat out of hell.

'Right, Mr Mayor,' he said with a voice turned into a nervous squeak, 'we'll be leaving you to get on with your business. I'm sure you would prefer this to be a private discussion.'

Cocklewell wanted to request, no *demand*, that the two of them stay, but words would not come to his suddenly constricted throat.

His son-in-law weighed up whether it would be best to risk the ire of the Mayor by going or the rage of the Matron by staying. 'I'll see you later,' he said to the speechless Mayor.

They pushed their way past the broad-shouldered Matron, who had eyes – murderous eyes – only for the Mayor. 'You,' she said, pointing at the quaking Cocklewell and managing to make that one word sound like a shot from a pistol. 'What the hell do you think you're up to?'

The Mayor moved his lips around his cigar, but no sound emitted from his mouth.

'There's only one way to deal with turds like you,' spat the Matron. 'I'm going to beat you to a pulp.'

But first she had to catch him. The Mayor started running round his large office like a man on the wall of death. They circled around and around his desk for five minutes until both were close to exhaustion.

It was the Matron who was the first to get second wind, and she gained on her quarry with a burst of acceleration that took her within two yards of him. She reached forward and grabbed hold of his braces, and as they stretched back in her hand she was forced to let them go because the desk was in her way. The Mayor was catapulted head first into the wall and his cigar was squashed against his face. He staggered back, grabbing an upright chair and holding it in front of him like a lion tamer. This, in the Matron's mind, was laying down

128

the ground rules, and she looked around for something with which she could arm herself.

Meanwhile, PC Shufflebottom was having problems getting past the picket line where an over zealous union official was attempting to point out the pros and cons of strike action. The constable finally got through after agreeing to wear a "Support Our Strike" sticker on his helmet and also to making a donation to the strike fund. He said that he would be able to spare a few coppers.

Nothing in Shufflebottom's training as a constable at Hendon Police College had prepared him for what he found as he stepped cautiously into the Mayor's office. This was how he later described the moment in court: 'I was proceeding on my usual police duties, what was to control and direct the traffic at the high street crossroads, when I was called to a disturbance at the Town Hall. I got there in all haste, and on arriving at the scene was informed by the Town Hall commissionaire that, and I quote, "there is a lady from hell what is in the Mayor's office." I proceeded up the stairs to the Mayor's chambers, and when I entered the office I found the man who I presumed to be the Mayor of our borough stretched out over his desk with his trousers down around his ankles. He was pinned down by the left hand of the accused what is here in the dock today, and in her right hand she had the Mayor's chain of office what she was whirling around like what I can only describe as a whip. The chain was landing with a whack on the Mayor's exposed behind which was black and blue by the time I arrived to take restricting action.'

What PC Shufflebottom's statement to the court did

not include was a full account of the farcical finale to the most incredible moments ever witnessed in the mayoral chambers. The constable stood rooted to the floor in the doorway when he first arrived, stricken with a mixture of fear and amazement at the sight of the Matron windmilling the chain of office on to the Mayor's bare backside. He was bare at both ends, because his ginger wig had slipped from his head. It was now caught around his groin area and looked as if he was wearing a Scotsman's sporran.

It was only when Matilda shoved him in the back that the stunned Shufflebottom stumbled into the office and prepared to make an arrest. He looked at the Matron and then at the Mayor, and chose the easy option of cautioning Cocklewell. The constable decided he could have him for indecent exposure.

'Not me, you idiot,' whimpered the Mayor, tears rolling down his fat cheeks. 'Lock this insane witch up before she kills me.'

'Anything you say will be taken down,' mumbled Shufflebottom, who produced his handcuffs with a well-rehearsed flourish and snapped one around the Matron's left hand. Then, in a state of some confusion, he locked the other half of the cuffs on to the right wrist of the Mayor, who was now suffering his worst nightmare of being attached to his 'lady from hell'. The Matron was still swinging the chain of office, and was now whacking it against Cocklewell's shoulders.

Her assault only ended when her leather-gloved grip slipped on the chain, which flew out of her hand and through the open office first-floor window. It landed around the shoulders of a union picket, who insisted it was a chain letter sent personally to him. He went off home wearing it.

Shufflebottom could not find the key to the handcuffs, and the Mayor had to suffer the indignity of being led through the picket line to the waiting Black Maria with his trousers still half dangling around his ankles and with his wig precariously placed on his head back to front. Cuffed to him was the Matron, sobbing with rage. The pickets, well aware of the Mayor's reputation as a molester of women, thought that he had been caught trying to have his wicked way with the Matron and he had to run a gauntlet of jeering strike protesters. It has to be said that there were one or two, equally aware of the Matron's 'Iron Maiden' reputation, who cheered *him*.

There was more humiliation still to come for Cocklewell. In a mix-up at the police station, the Matron was at first released and he was put into a cell. Shufflebottom finally got it sorted out, but not before the Mayor had nearly burst a blood vessel screaming his innocence.

Three magistrates, two women and a man, sat in judgement of the Matron to decide whether she should be sent for trial for causing grievous bodily harm. The male magistrate was on the Mayor's payroll, but his two colleagues belonged to the same women's guild as the Matron. They voted by two to one for the Matron to be bound over to keep the peace.

It was not quite what the battered and bruised Mayor had wanted. He had demanded that she should be sentenced to join a chain gang.

PC Shufflebottom was recommended for a bravery award.

The backlash of the Matron's assault was that it hardened the Mayor's resolve to close the hospital, and the Council issued an official twenty-eight days notice order for Haven to be shut down.

It was this news that triggered Dr Kilmore to summon Sydney Roper to organise another emergency meeting at the Crown and Anchor. It was the same gathering as before, with the addition of Clarence in his role as union representative. Tinkle and Matilda Thrush sat together with Clarence in the first row, with Roper, Francis Bigger, Bernie Biddle and stallholders Fred Apple and Peter Smith ranged behind them in the second row. Charlie Baron was stretched flat out on three chairs behind them, with Nurse May in attendance because he was convinced contractions were about to start.

Remembering how he had fallen off the stage the last time, Kilmore decided to address the gathering from the comparative safety of the floor. 'We have just one month in which to save the hospital,' he warned. 'Sadly, all our efforts so far have done nothing to force a change either of mind or of heart. I have called today's meeting in the hope that we can come up with an eleventh-hour solution to the crisis.'

Kilmore continued to keep his personal save-the-hospital plan to himself as a last resort. He preferred to throw the discussion open to see if anybody could come up with a better answer than the one he was keeping under wraps.

Clarence was first to respond. 'First of all,' he said, 'I would like to say on behalf of my brothers and sisters in the union how much we appreciate the efforts you are making to keep the hospital open and to rescue the jobs what is the livelihood of my members. Our union activity continues, but we are faced with an enemy what is unmoved by the disruption caused by our strike action.'

He reached into the inside pocket of his jacket and produced a rolled-up poster. 'Our comrades in the Bill Poster and Stickers union,' he explained, 'have come up with an idea to cover every wall in the borough with this wanted notice.' He unrolled the poster so that everybody could see the words that were ranged beneath a large picture of Mayor Cocklewell's face:

WANTED
FOR THE
MURDER OF THE
NATIONAL HEALTH
MAYOR COCK-UP

There were murmurs of approval around the room, except from Matilda. 'I'm sorry to throw cold water on what seems a bright idea,' she said, 'but for Mayor Cocklewell to see his face plastered all over the town would be a massive boost to his ego. I can assure you that he would consider it flattering, and he would put a macho interpretation on being called Mayor Cock-Up that would not have crossed normal minds.'

133

Kilmore invited more suggestions, and Sydney Roper was next on his feet. 'I think you've got to let me send the boys in,' he said. 'I know some geezers who are very tasty in the kneecapping department.'

'Come on, Sydney,' said Kilmore. 'Remember the Gandhi approach.'

'What about the Matron?' said Bernie Biddle.

'No, we can't get her involved in kneecapping,' said Roper. 'She's been bound over to keep the peace.'

'You know what I mean,' said Biddle. 'She was hardly a pacifist in her approach to the Mayor and where did it get her?'

'Well at least she had the satisfaction of giving him a good thumping,' said Roper. 'I understand the Mayor hasn't been able to sit down since, or maybe he's just standing for re-election.'

Nobody laughed. The situation was too serious for Sydney's laboured jokes to be appreciated.

Clarence started to say, 'I'd much rather, brothers and sisters...'

'Hallelujah,' chanted Francis Bigger.

'...that we left the Matron out of this discussion. She did what she saw as her duty, and now she's looking to us to continue where she left off.'

'Violence is not the answer,' said Kilmore. 'We need a more subtle plan.'

Francis Bigger raised both arms. 'Listen to Francis,' he said. 'We are going about this completely the wrong way. We have failed to reach the man's mind. Now let me try to reach his soul.'

Matilda laughed out loud. 'You've got a better

chance of getting through to the sole of his shoes,' she said. 'The man is soulless.'

'Ah, but he has never heard the preachings of Francis. Give me ten minutes alone with him and I will have him singing the praises of the hospital, just you see. Francis will have him converted to our cause in no time.'

'And you do mean converted,' said Roper.

'I'd like to convert him right between the posts,' added Bernie Biddle.

Kilmore would have liked extra time to consider something a little more positive, but the meeting was brought to a premature end by the moans and groans of Charlie Baron, who was starting phantom labour pains.

'Okay, Francis,' Kilmore said. 'We'll give you forty-eight hours to make the Mayor see the light or we will have to take more drastic action.'

'Thank you, my son,' said Bigger. 'Leave it to Francis. I will have the Mayor on his knees praying for the hospital to be kept open.'

Nurse May was mopping the perspiration from Baron's brow. 'We must get Charlie to hospital quickly,' she said. 'His waters have broken.'

'Don't worry,' said Sydney. 'Bernie and I will take him.'

So it was that Charlie Baron was lifted into the back of the hearse and driven to the hospital at breakneck speed. At the same time an ambulance was leaving Charlie's home with his wife heavily in labour. The ambulance and the hearse arrived simultaneously at Haven and both Charlie and his wife were rushed to the labour ward.

135

11

MATILDA made an appointment for the Right Reverend Francis Bigger to see Mayor Cocklewell on the pretext that he wanted to discuss matters of mutual interest. 'I don't know what you're thinking of, Tilly,' grumbled the Mayor. 'How can I 'ave mutual interest with a man who wears his collar back to front? You should have palmed him off to the charities committee.'

Matilda could play the Mayor like a violin. 'But he mentioned that the mutual interest was financial,' she said.

'Financial, eh?' he said, unconsciously patting his wig into place. 'That's interesting. Now I wonder what a man of the cloth could offer me in the way of inducement?'

'How about redemption for all your sins?' Matilda felt like saying, but made do with a shrug of the shoulders.

The Mayor did not have to wait long for his curiosity to be satisfied. Bigger made a grand entrance, blessing the commissionaire, the receptionist and the Town Hall cat before being shown into the Mayor's office. The commissionaire had thought he looked familiar, but could not place him; possibly because Francis was wearing the full regalia supplied along with his certificate from the 'Holier Than Thou' mail-order company: sky-blue cassock, cardinal's hat, dog collar and a gold-plated cross big enough to hang a coat on.

'Reet pleased to meet you, your fatherness,' Cocklewell said, trying hard to disguise the fact that he was extremely uncomfortable in the company of men of holy orders, who always reduced him to a fawning respect born of fear of their presumed power. 'It's an honour to make your acquaintance.'

'Yes it is, isn't it?' said Francis. 'You are no doubt wondering why I am giving you this audience.'

'Aye, that's quite true,' the Mayor said, 'I understand you want to discuss some matters, uh, financial.'

'Not me, my son, but somebody Up There,' Francis said, raising his eyes.

The Mayor looked heavenwards. 'From up there? You've got a message for *me*?'

'You are William *Septimus* Cocklewell, formerly of Grimestone Mansions, East Bradford?' Francis said.

The Mayor nodded, trying not to look stunned. Apart from Tilly who had seen his birth certificate, nobody knew his middle name; and there was nobody apart from his trusted Tilly who had known of his Grimestone Mansions background.

'I have to tell you, Mr Mayor,' said Francis, lowering his voice to reverential tones, 'that I have been gifted with special powers that make me the recipient of messages from the great beyond.'

Cocklewell was impressed and unnerved at one and the same time. He had had a secret fear of the occult ever since a gypsy, whose palm he declined to cross, had told him that one day he would have to answer for his meanness and that it would come like a bolt from the

137

blue. Suddenly Bigger's sky-blue cassock took on new meaning.

'You mean, you're in touch with the spirits?'

'Not when I'm on duty,' said Francis, 'but if you insist I'll have a Scotch, and while you're about it make it a large one.'

Matilda, listening in the outer office, winced. He had promised not to touch a drop until he had completed his assignment. A drunken Francis Bigger could blow the whole scheme. All the hours she had spent filling him in on everything there was to know about Cocklewell could be wasted, and her cover blown with it.

As the Mayor crossed to the cocktail cabinet, his mind was still full of concern about the message his visitor – his bolt from the blue – had received. 'Who's the message from?' he dared ask.

'Ah, that I cannot tell you,' ad-libbed Francis. 'It is a question only you can answer.'

The Mayor handed him his large Scotch and sat down. No sooner had he settled back into his chair than Francis was handing the glass back for a refill.

'You like a tipple, do you, your graceness?' Cocklewell said as he returned to the cocktail cabinet, this time bringing the whisky bottle back and placing it alongside the glass.

'Verily, verily and thrice verily,' chanted Francis, picking up the glass and sinking it in one backward tilt of his head. 'It helps me get in touch with the spirits, quite literally so to speak. This is the true wine of the saviour who founded the church of which I am privileged to be an ordained member.'

138

'Which church is that?' asked Cocklewell, who was a practising agnostic who had managed to avoid all matters religious while on his upwardly mobile climb. But now that he was at the top he was desperately seeking something to cling on to and to believe in, just in case it mattered when he eventually reached 'the other side'.

'The religious movement I belong to is called the Holier Than Thou Church. You will, of course, have heard of us. It was founded in Manhattan two years ago. We're very big on Wall Street.'

'Wall Street?'

'That's right. All the stock holders pray with us, you see, because we worship money.'

The Mayor was hooked. 'Money? You worship money? But that's the religion I've been looking for all my life.'

'Well search no more, my son, because we have found each other. Provided you believe a man should get his rewards here on earth and not have to wait until going to heaven then you have all the credentials necessary to become a member of our great church that boasts more followers than any other religion.'

'I'm with you all the way, your reverendness,' said the Mayor. 'Grab what you can while you can, that's my motto.'

'Well our first commandment is that you should love the dollar, or the currency of whichever country you're in, with all your heart and soul.'

'That's one commandment I'll never ever break,' Cocklewell said, lighting one of his huge cigars and blowing a smoke pattern in the shape of a pound-note sign. 'But, please, what is the message you bring? I must know.'

'Patience, my son,' said Francis. 'All in the goodness of time. You must first understand that I have to completely satisfy myself that you are the one and the same William Septimus Cocklewell for whom the special message is sent. It is easy to make a mistake unless you check all the personal facts. I once passed on a message from a departed husband to his wife, but it was meant for his mistress. From then on the wife went to bed every night wearing the stockings and suspenders that the deceased had said he was missing so badly.'

He poured himself another large Scotch.

'But why can't you just tell me what the message is, and see if I understand it?' said the Mayor, almost pleading.

'Because, my son,' said Francis, ready to throw the bait, 'there could be many thousands of pounds riding on your answer. I have to be sure you are who you say you are, and I must ask you some personal questions about your early life to verify it.'

The thought of many thousands of pounds swept away any concerns the Mayor might have had about answering a few questions.

'No problem, your fatherness. Fire away.'

'Right,' said Francis, reading from a sheaf of notepaper he had taken from his cassock pocket. 'First of all, do you know of a one-legged woman who used to work in a mill high on a hill in Bradford?'

'Mother!' exclaimed Cocklewell. 'That's my mother.

140

Used to push her up that hill every day in an orange box on wheels to get her to work. That's when I swore to make money my God, and so never have to crawl uphill again.'

'Very good,' said Francis. 'Now think carefully about this: were you ever promised a fortune by a mill owner but were let down by him?'

'Ee by gum, your fatherness, your information from whoever is on the other side trying to get in touch is uncanny. The owner of t'mill where my mother worked was so impressed by the way I pushed mother to work everyday that he promised he'd remember me in his will.'

Francis drained another glass. 'And what happened, my shun?'

'I were called to reading of t'will,' he said, 'and when solicitor read it out he said, "Just to prove that my client was of sane mind when making this last will and testament he wished to make it known that he could recall clearly young master Cocklewell here pushing his mother with the one leg up the hill to the mill every morning in an orange box on wheels. Yes, I remember him well." That were 'ow he remembered me in his last will and testament. Not a brass farthing, but I were remembered.'

A snigger coming into Bigger's throat was quickly turned into a cough, which of course called for another large Scotch as necessary lubrication. 'You could turn it into a shong about the mill, the hill and the will, Bill,' he said, quickly adding, 'I mean a hymn, of courshe.'

Cocklewell did not hear him. He was still back in the

141

past and trying to silently use his visitor's powers to reach the great beyond to send hate signals to the mill owner. He snapped back to the present.

'What about this message?'

'Jusht two more queshtionsh,' said Francis, now beginning to struggle to focus on the notes he had made when talking to Matilda.

'Can you name the two bats you ushed to torment?'

'Bats?' said Cocklewell, frowning so hard as he tried to remember that his wig visibly moved. 'I can't say as I can remember 'aving owt to do with bats.'

Francis squinted at his note. 'Shorry, I should have shaid cats.'

'Ah, Laurel and Hardy,' recalled the Mayor with a wicked grin. 'They were a black cat and a white cat that belonged to the man next door. I used to tie their tails with string and then attach other end to the knocker on t'door. Hilarious it were.'

He was suddenly gripped by fear. 'Hope message isn't from them two,' he said. 'They'd just tell me to get knotted.'

Francis emptied another glass to prepare himself for the coup de grâce.

'Now we come to the mosht shignificant question of all,' he said, pausing for dramatic effect, which was slightly spoiled by the fact that he was now slumping in his seat.

The Mayor sat on the edge of his chair in deep concentration, totally convinced he was in the presence of a man who could reach the spirit world. Trouble was Francis was in danger of drowning in it.

142

He made a supreme effort to ask the all-important question. 'Did you know a nush?' he asked.

'A nush?' said Cocklewell, scratching his head and dislodging his wig so that it was now perched diagonally across his head. 'A nush? What or who the 'eck is a nush?'

Francis held the notes right up to his eye, and just managed to make out the word 'nurse'.

'Shorry,' he slurred. 'I should have shaid nush.'

The Mayor, now in a state of extreme agitation, snatched the notes from Bigger. 'Nurse, you silly man,' he said. 'Nurse. Of course, Nurse McDonald. The only person who was ever kind to me when I were a lad. Used to call in to see mother, and would bring me a bun and sometimes a toy.'

He could now see her as clearly as if she was standing next to him, and he could smell the carbolic soap and starch. 'Aye, Nurse McDonald,' he said, tears springing to his eyes. 'Once gave me a shiny little red London bus for Christmas. That were when I first started dreaming of coming t'London to make my fortune. Nurse McDonald. Is she the one with the message?'

Francis was now slumped in his seat sound asleep. Cocklewell interpreted this as him being in a trance getting in touch with the great beyond.

Suddenly the telephone rang, and the Mayor was so startled that his wig bounced on his head. He stubbed out his cigar, and then in some trepidation picked up the telephone to hear the distant disembodied voice of a woman, clearly coming from 'the other side'.

'Is that you Wee Willie?' the voice asked with an eerie

143

echoing effect.

'It is me, Nursie,' said Cocklewell, realising straight away that it must be Nurse McDonald because she was the only person ever allowed to call him Wee Willie.

'I am coming to you from the great beyond thanks to the transmitting power of the Right Reverend Francis Bigger, och aye the noo.'

In the outer office, on 'the other side' of the wall, Matilda was under her desk with her head in the waste-paper bin in an effort to give the call more atmosphere. She had unilaterally decided on this drastic salvage action when she saw that the drunken Bigger had buggered it.

'I'm reet pleased to hear from you, Nursie,' said Cocklewell. 'How 'ave you been keeping?'

'Can't complain,' said Matilda in a Scottish voice borrowed from her favourite television series, *Doctor Finlay's Casebook*. 'Your mother sends her love, and says that her leg is much better.'

'Does she still need the orange box?'

'Not up here, silly. She's got her own chariot with a white horse.'

'Sounds greet,' said the Mayor. 'Mother never liked horses down here, 'cos father used to lose all his money on them.'

'I want you to know that your mother and father are proud of your achievements. You have done very, very well with your life, Wee Willie.'

Cocklewell's chest swelled so much that he nearly burst his braces. Francis Bigger was now snoring, but the Mayor was pleased that it did not affect the reception on the telephone. He had a perfect line, almost as if it were coming from the next room.

'His fatherness Francis Bigger mentioned summat about me coming into a fortune,' said the Mayor, his greed swamping his desire to reminisce with Nurse McDonald.

'Och aye, the money,' Matilda said. 'First of all tell me, Willie, is it true that you are planning to close down Haven Hospital?'

'Aye,' said the Mayor. 'It's got to come down to make way for a supermarket.'

'Oh dear, oh dear, oh dear,' Nursie's voice repeated in his ear.

'What's up?' said Cocklewell. 'You sound upset, Nursie. Those bloody cats aren't giving you aggravation, are they?'

'Och, no, it's just that we have a big problem. I'll have to report back to headquarters before I can tell you about the money.'

'But why can't you tell me now?' said the Mayor, almost having to shout to make himself heard above the increasingly loud snores emanating from Bigger's wide open mouth.

'All I can tell you is that if the hospital closes down you can forget the money. I don't know the full facts myself, but it's got something to do with a man who used to own the mill where your mother worked.'

'That old skinflint who remembered me in his will?'

'Be careful,' warned Matilda, alias Nurse McDonald. 'He is, I understand, the very man who could make you rich beyond your wildest dreams.'

145

'So the old so-and-so *did* find a way of taking it with him,' Cocklewell thought to himself. 'But if he's going to make me rich beyond my wildest dreams he would have to make me *exceptionally* rich because my dreams are extremely wild.'

He returned his attention to the conversation with Nurse McDonald in the great beyond.

'But what's all this got to do with the closing down of the 'ospital?'

'I can't answer that, except to say that you must allow it to remain open if you wish to one day receive the promised riches.'

Matilda looked out from the waste-paper bin to see that Francis Bigger was beginning to stir. She put her head back into the bin, and deliberately started to let her voice fade away. 'I'm sorry, but I must go now, Willie,' she said plaintively. 'I will return once it is clear that the hospital is to be spared from the bulldozers. Then, and only then, will I be able to tell you exactly how and when the money will be coming to you. Remember, whatever you do, *don't close the hospital.*'

'I hear you, Nursie,' said the Mayor. 'But just one thing before you go. How did an Irish lady like you get such a strong Scottish accent?'

Matilda's inventive mind went into overdrive. 'It's all to do with the person through whom I'm transmitting, so it is,' she said in as near as she could get to an Irish accent, borrowed from a young Irish comedian she had heard on television. 'It's the way I tell 'em, so it is. When the Reverend Bigger is in a trance, he thinks in Scotch, so he does. I must go now Wee Willie. Don't forget,

146

don't close the hospital, begorrah.'

As Matilda got out from under her desk and replaced the receiver, Bigger suddenly sat bolt upright.

'Well, my son, are you ready for your message?' he asked, returning to the world of sobriety into which he came and went as if in a non-stop revolving door.

'It has come over loud and clear, thank you,' said Mayor Cocklewell quietly.

'It has?' said a confused Francis. 'I've relayed everything, about Haven Hospital not to be closed under any circumstances?'

'So you did hear part of the conversation,' said the Mayor. 'Even though you were in that deep trance.'

'Uh, verily, verily and thrice verily,' said Francis. 'I heard only what I was meant to hear. The spirits have a strange way of working their wonders.'

Cocklewell was clearly shaken and moved by his experience, and now all he wanted was to be left alone so that he could do some quiet thinking.

He stood and shook Bigger warmly by the hand. 'Come, your fatherness, you must be exhausted. Let me accompany you to the mayoral car, and I will have my chauffeur drive you on to your next destination.'

Francis had a feeling that something close to miraculous had happened in the office that morning as he stood on his unsteady feet. He picked up the two-thirds empty bottle of whisky. 'I shall take this with me for medicinal purposes,' he said. 'It obviously has very special powers because I have put you in touch with the world beyond and you have got your message. That is a true miracle.'

147

The Mayor nodded his agreement, and Francis decided for one more punt as he was clearly in such a receptive mood. 'To help Francis carry on the work of Him above, can you see your way clear to giving me a few bob, on account sort of thing.'

Cocklewell called out to Matilda. 'His fatherness is just about to leave, Tilly,' he said. 'Take a 'undred pounds out of the petty cash tin and give it to him. Mark it down as being for a message delivery.'

Matilda handed the money in an envelope to Francis. 'I'll just see him to the mayoral car,' said Cocklewell. 'When I come back there's an urgent letter I want to dictate for the attention of 'aven 'ospital.'

As the Mayor led the still rocky Francis down the winding staircase, the right shoe of the man of the cloth got caught in the hem of his sky-blue cassock. He went into a forward roll, taking the Mayor with him and the pair of them somersaulted down the remainder of the stairs. The whisky bottle smashed, the contents soaking the Mayor's wig that came off during the fall.

They ended up in an untidy heap at the bottom of the staircase, with the commissionaire looking down at them. 'Got it!' said the commissionaire as he studied Bigger from a different angle. 'That's how you used to cower in the desert when Rommel was letting us have it. You're Frankie Bigun.'

The now bald-for-all-to-see Mayor stood up. 'You know his fatherness?' he asked.

'Know him?' said the commissionaire. 'He was the worst soldier ever to disgrace the proud reputation of the Desert Rats.'

148

'He was a chaplain?'

'Don't make me laugh,' said the commissionaire, laughing. 'Nearest he got to the chaplain was when he was trying to nick the altar wine. This is Private Frankie Bigun, the man we all knew as "King Con".'

The Mayor was now in a state of confusion as the fast sobering Bigger got to his feet and started to sidle towards the exit. 'So all that message bit was a con?' he said quietly, not wanting to believe it. 'So that wasn't Nursie I was talking to? There's no money coming my way? Mother hasn't got a chariot drawn by a white horse? Her leg isn't better?'

As if to confirm all the answers that the Mayor feared, Bigger was now doing his best to escape the clutches of the commissionaire.

'Does this mean you won't be making any further donations to the Holier Than Thou Church funds?'

Cocklewell snatched the envelope containing the hundred pounds from his hand. 'I won't be making this donation, either. Kick him out.'

The commissionaire took great delight in kicking Bigger down the Town Hall steps.

As he reached the bottom step, the Mayor cupped his hands around his mouth like a megaphone. 'By the way, your fatherness,' he shouted, 'next time you're in touch with the great beyond, tell t'mill owner that I'll not be remembering him in *my* bloody will.'

Matilda, oblivious of all that had got on downstairs, sat with her pen poised over her notebook ready to take down the most important letter she had ever looked forward to typing.

The Mayor was in a state of great agitation as he strode around the office searching for the right words, and she took this to be the nervous reaction to his message from Nurse McDonald.

'Reet, Tilly,' he said, 'get this down. 'To Mister C A Clutterbuck, 'aven 'ospital. This is to inform you that having given due thought and consideration to the twenty-eight day notice what I 'ave given you for the closing down of said 'ospital, I have now had a change of mind. This is to inform you, official like, that you will now close down 'ospital in twenty-one days from today's date. With kindest regards, etcetera etcetera, William Cocklewell, Mayor of this Borough.'

The Mayor stopped pacing and puffing on his cigar. 'Reet, Tilly, type that up and get it delivered straightaway by 'and.'

Matilda had not heard a thing since the letter's fourth sentence. She had fainted in her chair.

The Mayor looked at her. 'Poor Tilly,' he said. 'You've been overdoing it. You must take a break once we've got this 'ospital business over.'

Cocklewell then returned to his chair, and started to try to figure out how Francis Bigger had known so much about him. 'He really must have contacts on the other side,' he said aloud to himself. 'Can you hear me Nursie?'

12

THE TIME HAD arrived for Dr Kilmore to reveal his master plan to try to save the hospital. There were just twenty days left before the deadline for the closure, and it had to be now or never. Kilmore decided to drop a security screen on what he code-named OPERATION MINOR, which translated as Mayor In Need Of Rebuke. He shared his secret with just five other major players in the drama: Kenneth Tinkle, Matilda Thrush, Nurse May, Sydney Roper and Bernie Biddle.

He summoned them to a meeting at the local public park where they spread out in the front and back of Biddle's hearse, safe in the knowledge that they would not be overheard, except perhaps by the occupant of the coffin, the late Mrs Murgatroyd.

Kilmore, sitting in one of the two front passenger seats alongside Nurse May and Biddle, gave a quick resumé of the state of play. 'We have now played virtually all our cards and Mayor Cocklewell has trumped us every time,' he said. 'There is now only one course of action left open to us, and that is to make the Mayor unequivocally aware of the absolute necessity of a hospital in the borough.'

'Easier said than done,' said Matilda, lodged in the back of the hearse and feeling less than comfortable as she sat peering over the top of the coffin at Tinkle and Roper on the opposite side. 'What we have to realise is that in as much as the Mayor is concerned we are not dealing with a normal human being. The only necessity in his life is that there should be a bank and that it has several very large accounts in his name. A hospital means nothing to him.'

'Ah,' said Kilmore dramatically, 'but all that would change...' – and here he paused for maximum effect and then emphasised every word – ' ...*if the hospital saved his life.*'

He waited for his words to sink in. Biddle was struggling to take them on board.

'But 'ow can we save his life if his life ain't in danger?' he asked, vocalising the silent thoughts of the others at the meeting.

'Easy,' said Kilmore. 'We operate on him.'

There was a five-person chorus. 'Operate on him?' Even Mrs Murgatroyd might have been shocked into making herself heard.

'Yes, operate on him,' Kilmore repeated. 'At Haven.'

Dr Tinkle could not resist some heavy sarcasm, a specialised tone of language in which he was fluent. 'Oh, but of course,' he said, with a spread of his arms. 'Why didn't we think of this before? I mean, it's so glaringly obvious, isn't it?'

He mimed as if picking up a telephone and then talking into the receiver. 'Oh, is this Mayor William Cocklewell?' he said. 'It's Haven Hospital here. Surgery department. Would you mind popping in when you have a spare moment. We want to whip out an organ or two while you lie unprotesting and completely compliant on the operating table.'

Tinkle waited for the nervous laughter of the others

to die down before pointing at the coffin. 'We've got more chance of getting whoever's in there back to life than getting the Mayor to volunteer to come to the hospital for treatment,' he added.

'But who said anything about volunteering?' said Kilmore. 'Just listen to my plan, and then see what you think.'

'All right,' said Tinkle, with something less than conviction. 'You've got our undivided attention, particularly that of the man in the box. He's probably the only one who can see the full sense of what you're saying.'

'This ain't a man, this is Mrs Murgatroyd,' said Biddle, almost by way of introduction. 'We're going to have another go at burying her this afternoon.'

Kilmore now had everybody's full concentration, although he could not vouch for Mrs Murgatroyd. 'This is my plan,' he said. 'This afternoon I will give Matilda a specially concocted tablet that she must slip into the Mayor's tea sometime tomorrow morning. Within ten minutes of swallowing it he will have acute stomach pains. Matilda will get the Town Hall switchboard operator to ring immediately for an ambulance, an emergency call that will be intercepted by Sydney and Bernie.'

'But 'ow will we do that?' asked Biddle.

'I will go into the nuts and bolts in a minute,' said Kilmore. 'Let me give you the full outline first. You, Bernie, will be dressed as an ambulance driver, with Sydney as your assistant. I'll see to it that Clarence lets you "borrow" the third ambulance at Haven.'

'If 'e drives it anything like 'e drives this 'earse, we'll never find the bloody 'ospital,' said Sydney.

Kilmore ignored the aside. 'They will collect the Mayor in the ambulance and bring him to the Haven's operating theatre at top speed,' he said. 'Dr Tinkle and I will be waiting dressed in full surgeon gear, complete with masks to protect our identity.'

'Just a minute,' said a suddenly alarmed Tinkle. 'You seem to have forgotten an incey wincey little detail. We are doctors, not surgeons. I couldn't operate to save my life, or even the Mayor's life. You know how I hate the sight of blood.'

'Keep your hair on, Kenny,' said Kilmore. 'We won't be operating, just pretending to.'

'Like a game of doctors and nurses what we used to play when we were kids,' said Nurse May.

'Uh, sort of,' said Kilmore. 'Nurse May will simply give the Mayor an antidote after he *thinks* we have operated. But before then, while he's still in pain, we will get him to sign a form lifting the closure notice. Once the pain has gone, he will be so delighted that he will realise just how important the hospital is, and confirm the long-term future of the Haven.'

Tinkle was still sceptical. 'There's one other minor point you have forgotten,' he said.

'Yes, well this *is* Operation Minor,' said Kilmore. 'What have I forgotten?'

'Not what, but who,' explained Tinkle. 'Harmon Hardcastle, our mad surgeon. He is hardly going to say, "Come on in chaps, the operating theatre's all yours. Help yourselves to the scalpel and the cutting saw."'

154

Tinkle turned white even as he was thinking of it.

'This is why it is imperative that we carry out Operation Minor tomorrow,' Kilmore stressed. 'It's Hardcastle's day off, and there is nobody booked in for operations.'

'But that won't stop 'ardcastle coming in,' Nurse May said. 'He don't know one day to the next. He's even been known to sleep in the operating theatre.'

'Why, has he no home to go to?' asked Matilda.

'He's got an 'ome all right,' said Nurse May. 'Great big millionaire's gaff. Trouble is he don't know where to find it.'

'Leave the Hardcastle problem to me,' said Kilmore. 'I'll take care of that. What we must do now is to confirm that we all know exactly what we're doing.'

'At this moment in time,' said Tinkle, 'I think it safe to assume that only Mrs Murgatroyd knows exactly what her next move is.'

'With Biddle at the wheel, don't you bet on it,' said Roper.

'Right,' said Kilmore, rising above the banter, 'this is the plan of campaign. Matilda, you call into the hospital around about tea-time today and I will slip you the tablet. What time does he have his morning tea?'

'Whatever time I feel like making it for him,' she said. 'How does eleven o'clock suit you?'

'Fine,' said Kilmore. 'You, Bernie and Sydney, will collect the ambulance and a uniform each from Clarence at nine tomorrow morning. Park it outside my digs, and you, Sydney, go inside and wait for an emergency telephone call from the Town Hall.'

'But how will the telephone operator know what number to ring?' said Sydney. 'If there's an emergency, she will surely automatically ring either the 'ospital direct or 999.'

'I can fix that,' said Matilda. 'I'll give the number of the digs to the switchboard operator and tell her that in case of any emergency involving the Mayor, that is the number to ring.'

'Brilliant,' said Kilmore. 'Dr Tinkle, Nurse May and I will be waiting in the operating theatre from eleven thirty, and we'll be gowned and gloved ready for action. I'll make sure Clarence organises instant access for Sydney and Bernie to bring the Mayor straight to us without all the usual signing in formalities.'

Kilmore looked around at the blank faces staring back at him. He suddenly felt as if he might have got a better response from Mrs Murgatroyd. 'Well that's the plan,' he said. 'I know it's not quite foolproof...'

'Well it could fool me,' said Bernie Biddle.

'You can say that again,' said Roper.

'Well, it's the best I can think of at this eleventh hour,' added Kilmore. 'If none of you can come up with a better idea, then we've got to try it. It will be our last chance to save the hospital.'

'I can see holes in the plan,' said Matilda. 'But it's better than anything I can come up with. I vote that we give it a go.'

'I agree,' said Roper. 'We've tried everything else. Strike action, violence via the Matron, a bent safety report and Saint Francis trying to reach his soul. The only alternative now, as Dr Kilmore says, is to get him 'elpless in the operating theatre so that he appreciates just what the 'ospital is all about. Once he's on his back on the operating table, we'll have him by the balls.'

'Thank you, Sydney,' said Kilmore. 'Succinctly put. I will now put it to the vote. Those in favour of going ahead with Operation Minor?'

There was a unanimous show of hands. Only Mrs Murgatroyd abstained.

Bernie Biddle dropped off four of his six passengers until he was left with just Sydney Roper and Mrs Murgatroyd for company. 'Right Mrs M,' he said aloud, 'we've got one more port of call and then we'll take you to your funeral.'

He drove Sydney to his betting shop office in the high street. 'Come in and 'ave a bit each way,' said Sydney. 'I've got a tip on an 'orse that can't lose.'

'But you're the bookmaker, Syd,' said Bernie. 'You can't give me a winner if you're going to take my money. You'll have to pay me my winnings out of your own pocket.'

'Don't be daft,' said Sydney. 'I won't tell the other mug punters. The bet you and I 'ave I'll lay off with one of the big bookies. Come on. It's money for old rope. In fact that's the name of the 'orse we'll be backing. Old Rope.'

Biddle could never resist a bet, so he parked the hearse outside the betting shop. 'Won't be long, Mrs M, I'm just going to have a flutter on a dead certainty,' he said, and then he followed Roper inside.

'Right, come in to my back office,' said Sydney,

pushing his way past punters waiting for the start of the first race of the day. 'We've just got time to get our bet on. 'Ow much do you want to stake?'

'What are the odds?' asked Bernie.

'Ten to one,' said Sydney, looking at the board.

'Yeah, and if it's anything like your usual tips it will finish at twenty past four,' said Bernie.

'I'm telling you this is a racing certainty, pal,' said Sydney, noticing a change on the board. 'The odds have now lengthened on Old Rope to a hundred to eight, so you get a hundred smackers for every eight quid that you lay out.'

A wizened little old punter who regularly handed his hard-earned cash over to Roper's betting emporium every week just happened to be standing by the open door to the office, and he caught just enough of the conversation to convince him that he should put every penny in his pocket on Old Rope. That only amounted to eight pounds, but a win of a hundred pounds would be like something of a small fortune to him. He also whispered the news of Old Rope being a "racing certainty" to half a dozen of his cronies crammed into the tiny betting shop.

Bernie, meantime, was dragging his feet about taking a punt. How sure are you that it's going to win?' he asked. 'You know what a poor loser I am.'

'Well I've yet to meet a rich loser,' said Sydney. 'All I can tell you is that I've got this from the 'orse's mouth, well, at least from the mouth of the geezer who owns it. Said you could put your 'ouse on it.'

'I ain't got an 'ouse,' said Bernie.

'Then 'ow much do you want to put on the 'orse?' said Sydney, now getting irritated.

Bernie put his hands in his near-empty pockets. 'What do I get for eight pence?' he said.

'You can't expect me to put on an eightpenny bet,' fumed Sydney.

'Well, I only asked,' said Bernie. 'Can you lend me eight pounds until pay day?'

Sydney had done a lot of silly things in his time, but one of them was not lending money to punters. 'Do me a favour,' said Sydney. 'The first rule for a bookmaker is "only gamble with somebody else's money", so there's no way I can subsidise you. Haven't you got any more than eight pence?'

Bernie thought for a moment, and then remembered where there was five pounds. 'I'll be just two ticks,' he said. 'I've got five pounds on the dashboard of the hearse. It's the vicar's fee for seeing off Mrs Murgatroyd later this afternoon.'

As he arrived outside the betting shop, he found the unmissable frame of PC Shufflebottom planting a parking ticket on the windscreen of the hearse.

'You can't do that,' Bernie said, suddenly gripped by a smouldering temper that was about the only quick thing about him.

'Oh yes I can and I have,' said Shufflebottom. 'This is a no parking zone. The notices what are printed on the lamppost are clear enough.'

'But this is a hearse,' argued Bernie. 'I can park it where I like when I've got a customer on board.'

'Oh no you can't,' said Shufflebottom. 'If it was the

159

house of the person what is deceased then that would be a different matter. But this hearse is parked outside a betting shop what is in a no parking zone. So you have got a ticket, mate.'

Bernie worked his mind hard for a response. 'Well it was one of the last wishes of my customer that she should be allowed a final wager,' he said, even surprising himself at the speed with which he had come up with such a plausible story.

'Well you can put that forward as a written excuse when you send in your fine,' said Shufflebottom.

Action came quicker to Bernie than words ever did. He lashed out and knocked the constable's helmet, still carrying the strike support sticker, to the ground.

'Right,' said Shufflebottom, 'that's your lot.' He whipped out his handcuffs and there was no confusion or hesitation this time as he snapped them on to Bernie's wrists.

'You're nicked,' he said. 'I'm charging you for hassaulting a police hofficer in the course of his duty. Anything you say may be taken down and used in evidence against you.'

'But what about Mrs Murgatroyd?' Bernie shouted.

'You can call her as a witness if you so wish,' said Shufflebottom as he pushed and pulled the protesting Bernie in the direction of the nearby police station.

There was such a commotion that everybody in the betting shop had crowded out on to the pavement to see what was going on. Sydney, just about to telephone his hundred pound bet on Old Rope, replaced the receiver and went out to try to discover why his betting

160

shop was suddenly empty. He got outside just in time to witness Bernie Biddle being bundled off by PC Shufflebottom.

With a shrug of his shoulders and a shake of his head, Sydney turned and walked back into the betting shop just as the Tannoy announced: 'And the winner by six lengths is Old Rope.'

He was suddenly surrounded by cheering punters, led by the wizened old customer. If Sydney could have at that moment got his hands on a piece of old rope, he would have strangled Bernie Biddle.

It was moments after Sydney had paid out the winnings that Dr Kilmore happened to walk into the betting shop to give Roper the keys to his digs in preparation for Operation Minor.

Seeing that Sydney was depressed, Kilmore asked if there was anything he could do to help. 'There is as it 'appens, Doc,' said Roper. 'You see that 'earse out there, do us a favour and drive it down to the cemetery.'

He explained about Bernie's arrest and that Mrs Murgatroyd was still waiting to be taken to her last resting place. 'And another thing, Doc,' Sydney said. 'Having that 'earse stuck outside my betting shop is death for my business. Everybody thinks it's waiting there for me after the killing the punters have just made.'

Kilmore agreed to drive the hearse to the cemetery. Luckily, Bernie had left the key in the ignition, and the doctor drove off at a controlled speed in keeping with the occasion to which his cargo was destined.

161

He had got to within a mile of the cemetery when the engine of the hearse gave a sudden chug, and the vehicle coughed to a halt. Kilmore, well experienced in events like this, checked immediately with the petrol gauge. It was empty.

It is moments like this when good Samaritans are in short supply. Kilmore tried to thumb down passing motorists to give him a lift to the nearest petrol station, which was half a mile behind him. They all put their foot down the moment they saw a man waving his arms around alongside a hearse.

Finally, two building workers who had been watching the pantomime from high up on a scaffold, clambered down and offered to help. With Kilmore at the wheel, they kindly pushed from the front, and the hearse had a surprisingly smooth reverse run to the petrol station. The pump attendant tried not to look surprised to find a hearse being pushed into the foyer.

Meanwhile, Bernie Biddle was being released on bail from the police station. He arrived outside the betting shop to find the hearse and Mrs Murgatroyd missing, and immediately returned to the station to report that the hearse had been stolen and Mrs Murgatroyd kidnapped.

It was, of course, PC Shufflebottom filling in on desk duty. 'Can you first of all describe the motor vehicle,' said the constable.

'You saw it,' said Bernie. 'It's black, with white trimmed wheels. A twelve 'orsepower Rolls Royce.'

'It's pulled by twelve horses?'

'No, you great berk. Twelve horse power is the size

of the engine.'

'I see,' said Shufflebottom, making slow, copious notes. 'What was the registration?'

'D-E-D, one.'

'That sounds familiar. Didn't I have reason to apprehend you in that very vehicle last week?'

'I was on my way to a funeral,' said Bernie, anger and aggravation creeping up on him in equal layers.

'Right,' said Shufflebottom, 'this Mrs Murgatroyd. Can you describe her.'

'She was a little lady, about five foot two inches tall,' said Bernie. 'I would guess she was aged about eighty-odd. She was a widow.'

'What was she wearing when you last saw her?'

'A shroud.'

'A shroud?'

'A shroud.'

'But ain't that what they put on people what is dead?'

'She is dead.'

Shufflebottom gripped his pencil so tightly that it broke. Ever since he had first considered joining the police force he had always wanted to get involved in solving a murder. 'And how did she die?' he asked, trying to keep the quiver of excitement out of his voice.

'Old age, I suppose,' said Bernie, not understanding where all these questions were leading.

'A likely story,' said Shufflebottom, reaching across the desk and grabbing Bernie by the wrists. 'I'm arresting you on a charge of being an accessory before or after the murder of Mrs Murgatroyd. Now all we need is to find your accomplice who has the body hidden in a hearse.'

At this moment the duty sergeant returned from his tea break, and immediately recognised Bernie as the undertaker's assistant who had been charged with assaulting PC Shufflebottom just before he went to the canteen.

'What's going on Shufflebottom,' he said. 'You two aren't having a return match, are you?'

'He has been an accessory in the kidnapping of a widow what is known as Mrs Murgatroyd,' the constable reported. 'His accomplice has driven off with her in a hearse.'

An all-cars call was relayed across the borough, and so it was that Kilmore – driving the hearse and Mrs Murgatroyd – was apprehended just a few hundred yards away from the cemetery gates.

'We have reason to believe that you have Mrs Murgatroyd in there,' the police car driver said, as he forced Kilmore to spread his legs while lying flat against the bonnet of the hearse.

'That's right,' said Kilmore. 'She's in the hearse.'

'Ah, so you admit it,' said the police officer triumphantly. 'I've heard all about you. My mate what works in the hospital mortuary said that you're one of them dead body lovers.'

'I'm nothing of the sort,' Kilmore said, his nose flattened to the bonnet. 'I'm a doctor employed at Haven Hospital and I am trying to get poor Mrs Murgatroyd to her final place of rest.'

'That's what they all say,' said the police constable. 'You are now going to accompany me to the police

164

station for further questioning. Meantime I am charging you with the theft of a vehicle, being one black hearse registration number D-E-D One, and the suspected abduction and possible murder of a Mrs Murgatroyd, of no fixed abode.'

'She does have an abode,' Kilmore said, 'if only you would let me get her there. She belongs in the cemetery.'

'And so do you, pal,' growled the police officer as he snapped handcuffs on to Kilmore's wrists and led him to the police car. His colleague drove the hearse, and together they headed – along with Mrs Murgatroyd – to the police station.

It was another two hours before a fuming funeral director Ivor Bodie arrived at the station to verify the story being jointly told by Kilmore and Biddle. He identified the body as being Mrs Murgatroyd, and the funeral procession at last set off for the cemetery, with a police escort to clear the way.

It was the second most exciting day in the previously uneventful life of Mrs Murgatroyd.

13

HARMON HARDCASTLE, a genius of a hospital surgeon, unfortunately had a memory span that lasted no more than ten minutes. 'Hi, I'm Al Zheimer,' was how he would introduce himself to colleagues and patients alike. It was funny the first time he said it, a little less funny the second time and then ceased to be even slightly amusing when he repeated it every ten minutes.

Everybody at the hospital was aware of Harmon Hardcastle's progressive dementia, and they went out of their way to help him continue his brilliant career. There were few surgeons in the world who could match him for speed either of diagnosis or of incision. He could perform a complicated transplant operation with a swiftness and a sureness that confounded equally experienced colleagues, and minor operations were completed as quickly as it took some people to tie a pair of shoelaces.

It was said by his peers that to watch him at work cutting, stitching, slicing, sawing and repairing was on a par with witnessing Horowitz at the keyboard or Fanny Craddock in the kitchen. He was an absolute master.

Undoubted genius that he was, there were, however, drawbacks. He had been known to carry out three operations on the same patient in three hours, removing his spleen, replacing it and then removing it again before any of his colleagues around the table had realised he had completed even the first operation.

Then, of course, there was the famous time when he misplaced his watch. It was eventually found in the stomach of a patient on whom he had operated, and who later complained of a nervous tick.

But generally speaking, Oxford-educated Hardcastle was considered just about untouchable inside the operating theatre. It was away from it that he could prove something of a worrying liability.

He was the quintessential eccentric Englishman, who belonged to a dying breed. Since his beloved wife, Agatha, had passed on after forty-three years of marriage, the 68-year-old surgeon had found it increasingly difficult to cope with the modern world. He had to be moved out of his enormous mansion in Hampstead because he kept getting lost inside the house, and his major problem since switching to a three-roomed apartment in Chelsea was finding it.

His first love had always been driving, and he was a familiar figure throughout the borough with his unmistakeable dark green 1950s Bentley. But his driving licence had been revoked because he continually ignored the new one-way system, and it had all come to a head when he forced one of Ivor Bodie's funeral processions to back up for a mile while he was blowing his horn furiously and waving for them to get out of his way.

The hospital went to the expense of hiring a chauffeur for him, but he could never remember what he looked like and he was continually climbing into the backs of the wrong cars.

It had reached the stage with Hardcastle where he needed to have a large cardboard label tied to the lapel of his jacket which read, HI, I'M HARMON. IF FOUND WANDERING, PLEASE RETURN ME TO HAVEN HOSPITAL. THANK YOU.

While everybody felt sorry for Harmon because of his gradually worsening condition, he himself was unfailingly cheerful and was often to be seen talking away to himself and laughing out loud as he exchanged memories with his departed wife, who he was convinced was still at his side.

Hardcastle amused himself and Agatha by telling old jokes that he thought were fresh off the press. It was his contention that had he not followed his father, grandfather and a long line of ancestors into the precise and disciplined world of medical surgery, he would have been a music hall comedian. He considered the operating theatre his stage, and always tried to be entertaining while carrying out his work. Hardcastle was proud of the nickname that had been hung on him by his colleagues. It was based on the name given to one of his boyhood idols, the former world champion boxer Jimmy Wilde, who was known as 'The Ghost with a Hammer in his Hand.' Hardcastle had been dubbed, 'The Great Entertainer with a Scalpel in his Hand.'

Patients wheeled in to see him for treatment and diagnosis would find it more disconcerting than amusing to have the man who was to operate on them telling them what he thought were original 'good news,

168

bad news' jokes. 'I've got good news and I've got bad news, Mrs Smith,' he would say. 'The good news is that the operation to remove your right leg was a total success. The bad news is that I should have cut off the left leg.'

Because he could remember little of the present, he spent much of his time mentally in the past and it was nothing unusual for him to discuss such matters as the bombing of Pearl Harbor and the Wall Street Crash as if the events had just recently happened. It often led to some very confusing conversations, and one patient was naturally quite concerned when, on the eve of an operation to have a growth removed, Hardcastle talked intently to him about his schooldays and about how he had hated his maths teacher with a vengeance. The patient just happened to be a mathematics teacher at the local grammar school. He fainted after what was in fact a perfectly successful operation when Harmon told him, 'I've got good news and I've got bad news for you. First the good news. I've had to cut off both your feet. The good news is that your slippers fit the man in the next bed.'

This detailed background on Harmon Hardcastle will explain why Dr Kilmore was anxious not to have him anywhere near the operating theatre when the Mayor was brought in, and so it was that he dashed away after paying his final respects to Mrs Murgatroyd to visit the surgeon at his Chelsea apartment.

Kilmore was aware from previous visits that he had to be patient once he had rung the doorbell. He knew that inside Harmon would be first of all answering the telephone and then taking some time to find where the door was situated so that he could open it.

When he found Kilmore standing on his doorstep his face broke into a welcoming smile, and he pushed a button in his pocket that lit up the multi-coloured bow tie that he always wore. 'My dear boy,' he said, shaking Kilmore warmly by the hand. 'How good to see you. I'm Al Zheimer. Come on in. Agatha and I have been expecting you.'

Kilmore knew that he had not the slightest idea who he was, and so he prompted his memory. 'I'm James Kilmore, a doctor on the staff at Haven Hospital,' he reminded him, even though they had seen each other only the previous afternoon.

'Kilmore?' said Hardcastle, bidding him to take a seat on a huge 1930s sofa that had been transferred from the mansion and almost filled the lounge. 'Kilmore? Used to work with a young doctor called Kilmore, didn't I, Agatha? At Haven. Ever come across him?'

Kilmore thought it best to just nod.

'Now then, young man, what's it going to be?' Harmon asked, pushing the button in his pocket again and this time making the bow tie whirl. Always the entertainer. 'A quick snifter, or a cup of Agatha's finest Malaysian tea? Her own special brew, don't you know. She was taught how to make it when we were working in the same hospital in Malaysia. Ever been there?'

Kilmore shook his head.

'Wonderful place. And the gals. God. Pretty enough to knock your eyes out.'

He stopped and looked hard at Kilmore as if he was seeing him for the first time. 'Hello, young man,' he said, offering his hand. 'I'm Al Zheimer.'

Kilmore took his chance to try to explain what he was doing there. 'Mr Hardcastle, I am here from Haven Hospital to remind you *not* to report for work tomorrow because it's your day off.'

'That's awfully decent of you to come all the way out here to Hampstead to tell me that,' said Hardcastle, suddenly raising his voice. 'Did you hear that, Agatha? I've got tomorrow off.'

He thought an explanation was necessary. 'She's in the kitchen making us some tea,' he said. 'Wouldn't want you to think I'm potty.'

Hardcastle, whose carefully groomed jet-black hair from his youth was now a shaggy white, looked at Kilmore and shook his head. 'So you work at Haven, eh? Remarkable coincidence. So do I. One of the great hospitals. D'you know a Dr Kilmore? You look like his twin. Incredible. I once delivered four sets of twins on the same day when I was working in Malaysia.'

Kilmore took a notice from his jacket pocket on which were printed the words: THIS IS MY DAY OFF. I DO NOT HAVE TO GO TO HAVEN HOSPITAL TODAY.

'What I would like to do, Mr Hardcastle,' he said, 'is pin this notice on your jacket, so when you wake up in the morning it will remind you to relax and spend the day at home.'

He handed the notice to the Great Entertainer, who read it aloud. '"This is my day off. I do not have to go to Haven Hospital today." Well knock me down with a feather and tickle my fanny, as the actress said to the bishop, I could have sworn I had

171

been to the hospital today.'

'You have been in today,' Kilmore explained patiently, 'but this notice refers to tomorrow.'

Hardcastle studied the notice again. 'Sorry, old boy,' he said, 'but you're wrong. It quite clearly states "I do not have to go to Haven Hospital *today*."'

'Fair enough,' said Kilmore, knowing when he was beaten. 'But before I go I will pin it on your jacket so that you read it first thing tomorrow.'

Hardcastle reached out, and warmly shook Kilmore's hand. 'Hello young man, I'm Al Zheimer.'

Kilmore took this as a signal that he was best getting back to the hospital to make final arrangements for Operation Minor. 'Well I must be off now, Mr Hardcastle. It's been a pleasure talking to you.'

'You've got to go already?' said Hardcastle. 'But you've only just arrived. Can't you stay for a cup of Agatha's tea? Malaysian, you know. Her own brew.'

'I'm sorry,' said Kilmore. 'I've got to get back to Haven Hospital.'

'That's a coincidence. I was going there today but I've just found out that it's my day off. Quite unexpected.'

He held out his hand. 'Well, it's been a pleasure for Agatha and I to meet you Mr... uh...?'

'Dr Kilmore.'

'Oh, no. I'm Harmon Hardcastle. Kilmore is a young doctor at Haven. Come to think of it, you look just like him.'

Kilmore spotted Hardcastle's jacket hanging over a chair, and he pinned the reminder notice on to the lapel.

'I'll show you out,' said the surgeon, opening the door to the airing cupboard.

He put a friendly arm round Kilmore's shoulders as they reached the front door at the second time of asking. 'I've got good news and I've got bad news for you, young man,' he said. 'The bad news is that you've got syphilis.'

Kilmore found himself asking, 'And what's the good news?'

'You've also got Alzheimer's disease, so you'll quickly forget that you've got syphilis.'

The Great Entertainer spun his bow tie and lit it at the same time as he let Kilmore out of the door, and he was laughing aloud as he returned to Agatha and the world of his own.

As Kilmore made his way to his bicycle he pondered on how people at the hospital felt sorry for Harmon Hardcastle. Yet he could not remember when he had last been in the company of somebody as genuinely happy with life.

He just wished he had been able to taste that cup of Agatha's Malaysian tea.

It was while cycling through heavy early evening traffic along the Thames Embankment from Hardcastle's Chelsea home that Kilmore suddenly remembered that he had not handed the pain-inducing tablet to Matilda Thrush. He had got caught up in the Mrs Murgatroyd funeral drama, and it had completely slipped his mind. Now he needed to contact urgently either Tinkle or Nurse May to tell them where the tablet was and to get it to Matilda.

Kilmore glanced up at Big Ben and saw that it had just turned six o'clock. That meant he was too late to catch Tinkle, who would be on his way back to the digs after his nine-hour session on casualty department duty. He knew that Nurse May would be relaxing in her room at the nurses' hostel before starting her night shift at the hospital, and so he decided that he would have to trust her with the responsibility of collecting and delivering the tablet.

He turned left and cycled down towards Ludgate Circus where he found a public phone box on the corner of Fleet Street. After placing his bicycle up against a wall where he could keep an eye on it, he went to the kiosk to find that vandals had broken all the windows and that the door had been removed from its hinges. He was relieved to find that at least the telephone was in working order.

It was one of the old-fashioned 'A' and 'B' button telephones that were about to be phased out. He dropped in his last four pennies, and dialled the number of the nurses' hostel. The chilling voice of the supervisor, Miss Ironknickers answered. It was a voice so cold you could have frozen a hot potato on it.

Kilmore pushed button 'A' and as the four pennies clinked down into the coin container he put on his poshest voice. 'Good evening, ma'am, may I please speak to Nurse May,' he said.

'No you cannot,' came back the icy reply. 'No gentlemen callers after six o'clock. That is the rule of this hostel.'

'But I need to speak to her really urgently,' protested Kilmore, who found himself talking to a dead telephone as the supervisor pulled out the plug on the hostel switchboard.

He was in the mood to continue where the vandals had left off. All he had in change was a two bob coin. He crossed Fleet Street to a newsagents, bought himself an *Evening Standard* for fourpence, and got plenty of coppers in his change. This took just five minutes, but by the time he returned to the kiosk there was somebody on the telephone, and a queue of three other people waiting.

Kilmore got on the end of the queue and overheard without meaning to a quartet of one-sided telephone conversations. They ranged in subject from what the caller should wear for a party at the weekend, an excuse for being late home that night, a tearful breaking off of an engagement and, the caller before him, threatening to smash somebody's head in if they ever went near his girlfriend again. At last, after a twenty minute wait, it was his turn to make a call, and now there were five people queuing behind him.

This time when he got through and pushed button 'A' at the sound of Miss Ironknickers, he pinched his nose and said in a high-pitched voice: 'Hello, may I please speak to Nurse May.'

'Who is this calling?' asked the supervisor.

'This is her mother speaking,' Kilmore said.

The five people queuing behind him could not believe the cabaret to which they were being treated.

Kilmore heard the extension ringing, and then Nurse

May answered. 'Hello Goldilocks,' he said, 'Daddy Bear here.'

Nurse May was quickly alert, even though she had been dozing on her bed. 'Careful Daddy Bear,' she warned. 'The big bad wolf has got big ears.'

'The big bad wolf has got big ears?' Kilmore repeated before he realised that Nurse May was sending him a coded warning that Miss Ironknickers could be listening in on the switchboard.

'Oh, I understand,' he said, switching back to the female impersonation. 'Now listen, darling, it's mummy here. The tablet that needs to be given to our cat Matilda is in a small blue envelope inside the red plastic cup in the staff room medical cabinet. Do you follow me, my dear?'

'Yeah, I think so,' said Nurse May. 'It's inside a red envelope in the blue plastic cup.'

'No, silly,' Kilmore said in his own voice. 'In a blue envelope inside the red cup. Blue envelope, red cup. Got it?'

'Okay, Mummy,' she said. 'What d'you want me to do with it?'

'Give it to Matilda,' Kilmore said, switching back to his "mummy" voice.

'Where do I find her, Mummy?' asked Nurse May. 'I ain't got no idea where she lives.'

Kilmore kicked the front of what remained of the kiosk in frustration.

A burly, familiar-looking on-leave sailor, waiting next in line, rapped him on the shoulder. 'Oi, pal,' he said in a menacing voice, 'leave some of the kiosk for us to use, you bloody vandal.'

176

The doctor waved his apologies. 'For goodness sake, Goldilocks, use your gumption,' he said in his normal voice. 'When we've finished this call, ring the Town Hall and ask the night porter for Matilda's address. Tell him you're her sister.'

'Her sister? But I don't look anything like her,' said Nurse May.

'It doesn't matter on the telephone!' he shouted, punching at the one remaining pane of glass in the kiosk which shattered on to the pavement. 'Just get it sorted out.'

He dropped the receiver as he was suddenly hauled backwards out of the wreck of the kiosk by the sailor, who cracked him with a perfect straight right to the nose. 'Get out of there, you perverted maniac,' he said. 'Now make yourself scarce before I call the police to report you for wrecking the telephone box.'

Kilmore, blood seeping from his only recently mended nose, needed no second bidding to escape from the clutches of the sailor who he was convinced was carrying out a vendetta against him.

He looked along Fleet Street to find a number 15 bus approaching a request stop. He raced to the stop with his arm out, jumped on board and ran up the stairs, dabbing at his bleeding nose with a handkerchief.

Kilmore had gone six stops towards his destination when he looked down and noticed that he was wearing bicycle clips.

Back at Ludgate Circus, an on-leave sailor was seen happily pedalling a racing bike towards Blackfriars Bridge.

When Kilmore finally arrived back at the hospital, he found a fretting Nurse May pacing back and forth in the foyer. 'What 'appened to your nose?' she asked as he came through the sliding doors.

'Don't ask,' he said. 'Has Matilda got the tablet?'

Nurse May shook her head. 'Did you say a green envelope in a pink cup or a yellow envelope in a brown cup?' she asked.

This was all Kilmore needed to round off his day. 'D'you mean you haven't passed the tablet on to Matilda?' he said through gritted teeth and in a half whisper in case there were any unwanted ears flapping nearby. 'Blue envelope, red cup.'

'Well don't blame me,' said Nurse May. 'I couldn't see anything in your rotten old medical cabinet. No envelope, no tablet. No nothing.'

Kilmore raced to the lift, and pressed the button for the second floor. He was in too much of an agitated state to realise that the lift was going down to the basement.

He came charging out and raced blindly down the corridor. When he came to the door where the staff room should have been he became almost apoplectic when he read the sign MORTUARY.

Kilmore kicked the door in frustration, just as the mortuary attendant returned from his evening tea break. He took one look at Kilmore, holding a blood-stained handkerchief to his nose and wearing bicycle clips, and turned and ran back down the corridor.

Five minutes later, the crazed doctor could be found rifling through the medical cabinet in the staff room. Nurse May was right. There was no sign of the blue

178

envelope containing the tablet. Just an empty red plastic cup.

Thoroughly dejected, Kilmore went to the staff telephone and rang the digs he shared with Tinkle to tell him that Operation Minor was off. He had got the tablet on a special prescription, and it would arouse too many suspicions if he asked for a repeat.

'Hello?' a breathless Dr Tinkle answered.

'Kenny,' Kilmore said, 'it's Jim. Operation Minor is off.'

'What?' said Tinkle, 'But why? We're all up for it, aren't we Matilda my sweet?'

Kilmore could hear Matilda in the background, equally breathless. 'You can say that again, my darling,' she said. 'Yes, we're up for it.'

'But the tablet has gone,' said Kilmore. 'Somebody's taken it.'

'Of course,' said Tinkle, casually. 'I have.'

'What d'you mean, *you* have?' said Kilmore. '*You've* taken the tablet? Are you mad? That will give you terrible stomach pains.'

'No, silly man,' said Tinkle. 'I've taken it, as in taken it. I've handed it over to Matilda because you weren't around when she called into the hospital.'

The meaning of what Tinkle was saying slowly sank into Kilmore and he felt a wave of relief wash over him.

'Kenny,' he said, 'I could kiss you.'

'No wonder you're called Dr Strangelove,' Tinkle replied. 'Anyway, I'm getting all the kisses I need right here, thank you very much.'

Operation Minor was back on.

14

SYDNEY ROPER, ambulance man for the day, nearly jumped out of his skin when the telephone rang in the lounge at Kilmore's digs. He had been anticipating a call at around eleven-fifteen, but this was twenty minutes early. 'Emergency ambulance service,' he said into the receiver, holding a handkerchief over the mouthpiece because that is what he had seen them do at the pictures.

'This is the Town Hall,' a panic-driven woman's voice announced. 'Come quickly. I think the Mayor could be dying.'

'We're on our way, missus,' Sydney said with as much urgency in his voice as he could muster.

'Is there anything I can be doing to ease his pain?' the switchboard operator asked.

'Uh, you've got me there, missus,' said Sydney. 'Why not try my old mum's recipe and give him a cold bath. We'll be with you in two ticks.'

Sydney raced outside and signalled to Bernie Biddle to start up the ambulance, which was double parked alongside the unoccupied hearse. He jumped into the front passenger seat. 'Okay, my son,' he said. 'Let it rip.'

Bernie's eyes were wide with excitement. He had always dreamed of driving either a fire engine or an ambulance through the streets with alarm bells ringing and going like the clappers. It was a whole new exciting world after all the sedate stuff in the hearse.

They went powering around the first bend on their

way to the Town Hall just as milkman Jack Waters was reversing to start deliveries on the opposite side of the street. The ambulance side swiped his battery-powered milk float. Nobody was hurt, but there was broken glass flying everywhere and both Bernie and Sydney were smothered in milk that splashed through the open window of the ambulance. Worse still, jagged glass tore into the wheels of the ambulance and all four tyres were punctured.

Sydney, milk dripping from his temporary uniform, jumped out and surveyed the damage. 'Bloody blimey,' he said. He turned to the milkman, who was drenched in what he should have been delivering. 'Sorry, pal,' said Sydney. 'Complete accident. We'll sort it out later. Must dash. We're on an emergency call.'

'The float's still working,' said the milkman. 'You could take that.'

Another time Sydney would have laughed at the thought of putting the Mayor on the back of the milk float, but he had too big a crisis on his hands. 'Thanks a lot, but I've got a better idea.'

Bernie was staring blankly at the wreckage of broken bottles and the punctured tyres.

'Quick,' Sydney said to Bernie, grabbing a stretcher from the back of the ambulance. 'We've got to leg it back to the digs.'

'What are we going to do there?' asked Bernie, quickly wishing that he hadn't opened his mouth.

'There's only one thing for it,' said Sydney. 'We'll have to take your hearse.'

And so it was that a hearse turned up at the Town

Hall, with two milk-stained ambulance men on board.

Sydney picked up the rolled stretcher, and they raced into the foyer. The commissionaire gaped when he saw Sydney in his ambulance man's uniform. He was a regular punter at the betting shop.

'You doing this to win a bet?' he said.

'No, I'm helping out during the strike,' Sydney said off the top of his head. 'Where's the Mayor?'

'He's having a cold bath,' said the commissionaire. 'Miss Jenkins is with him.'

'Miss Jenkins?' said Sydney. 'Where's Miss Thrush?'

'Haven't a clue,' said the commissionaire. 'Haven't seen her since the tea break this morning.'

Sydney and Bernie were shown downstairs to the plunge bath that was alongside the swimming pool, which was for the exclusive use of councillors. The Mayor was sitting fully clothed in the bath, turning blue as his teeth chattered. He was crying with pain.

'Help me,' pleaded the Mayor. 'Please help me.'

'The cold bath doesn't seem to be doing any good,' Miss Jenkins said. 'He's still in a bad condition.'

'Right,' said Sydney, 'leave it to us.'

He unrolled the stretcher and took three minutes pondering which way up it should be. Bernie, meanwhile, was helping the shivering, pain-racked Mayor out of the bath.

Sydney placed the stretcher on the floor, and the Mayor lay down on it, his hands clasped to his gigantic, soaking-wet stomach.

Perspiration sprouted from the brows of both Sydney and Bernie as they tried to lift the stretcher off the floor.

182

After several attempts to get lift-off, Sydney came to a decision. 'It's no good your worship' he said to the Mayor. 'You'll 'ave to 'elp. Place your legs either side of the stretcher, and put your feet on the ground. Then we'll manoeuvre you up the stairs.'

With the Mayor sliding up and down the stretcher, they managed to get him back up to the foyer where the commissionaire helped them carry him down the Town Hall steps. Cocklewell saw the hearse waiting at the bottom of the steps. He let out a loud wail, and shouted: 'I'm coming to join you, Nursie.' Then he went into a dead faint. Passers-by seeing him being pushed into the back of the hearse quickly relayed the story that the Mayor was dead.

With Bernie at the wheel and driving in his best Stirling Moss style, the hearse sped off in the direction of the hospital. He had just reached the crossroads by the bus depot when he was forced to stop with a screech of tyres by the outstretched arms and mountainous frame of traffic duty policeman, PC Shufflebottom.

'Who d'you think you are, Stirling Moss?' he said sarcastically as he leaned through the window of the hearse. 'I'm going to give you a ticket for speeding and driving in a manner dangerous to the public.'

'But we've got the Mayor in 'ere,' said Sydney, sitting in the back trying to comfort the almost comatose Cocklewell.

Shufflebottom peered into the back. 'What's up with him then? Has he snuffed it?'

'We're taking him to the 'ospital,' said Sydney. 'He's

in desperate need of emergency treatment.'

'I'd say it's a bit late for that if he's in a hearse,' said Shufflebottom. 'I think you'd better open the back and let me have a look at him. For all I know, you could be up to your kidnapping lark again.'

The Mayor briefly came out of his stupor, and looked up through half-closed eyes to make out the giant head of PC Shufflebottom and the 'Support the Strike' sticker still on his helmet. Cocklewell was convinced he was in purgatory.

Even Shufflebottom was able to detect that the shade of blue on the Mayor's face was not quite what it should be. 'This man is sick,' he pronounced. 'He shouldn't be in a hearse. He should be in a hospital.'

'That's where we're trying to take him, you blithering idiot,' said an exasperated Sydney.

'No need for that sort of talk, sir,' the constable said. 'Careful, or I'll have you for what could be constituted as verbal abuse.'

He looked back at the Mayor, whose teeth were now chattering like castanets and whose lips were blue.

'I don't like the look of this,' he said. 'I am ordering you to proceed to the hospital forthwith, and just to make sure you don't try any of your body snatching larks I will accompany you.'

Shufflebottom climbed into the passenger seat, and so it was that ten minutes later a hearse came speeding into the hospital car park with a squeal of tyres, and containing one agonised Mayor, two milk-stained part-time ambulance men and one strike-supporting police constable.

The Mayor was quickly transferred to the hospital lift where Clarence, with a nudge, nudge, wink, wink, accompanied them to the emergency operating theatre on the first floor.

Kilmore and Tinkle were already gloved, masked and in their green surgeon's gowns when Mayor Cocklewell was wheeled in. They gave a double take when they saw PC Shufflebottom accompanying the patient. Kilmore put on his most officious voice. 'Right, that's as far as you all go,' he said. 'We do not want anybody in the operating theatre who is not authorised.' He slammed the theatre door shut on Shufflebottom, Clarence, Sydney and Bernie, trying to block out the thought that there was an almost overpowering stench of sour milk.

Both doctors were shocked by the effects of the tablet. 'You'd better get that antidote ready pretty damn quick, Nurse,' he said.

'Antidote?' said Nurse May. 'I ain't been given no antidote.'

'What d'you mean, you haven't been given one?' said Kilmore in a panic. 'It was in the blue envelope in the red...'

His voice trailed away as he worked out what had happened. Matilda had taken both tablets, and she had obviously slipped the wrong one to the Mayor, judging by his condition.

'There's only one thing for it,' said Kilmore, rolling up his sleeves ready for action.

'What's that?' said a wild-eyed Tinkle.

'We've got to operate.'

'What... us... you, me... operate?' said Tinkle, his voice going up and down the scale like a piccolo.

'It's all right,' Kilmore said, as reassuringly as possible in a bid to snap Tinkle out of his panic attack. 'We're not going to cut him open. We're going to pump him out. Nurse, the hose and warm water, please.'

'They had the Mayor bent forward and were just about to feed the tube down his throat when the door of the operating theatre swung open. Walking in as calmly as if on a stroll through the park came Harmon Hardcastle. He was gowned, gloved and masked for work.

'Good day,' he said. 'I'm Al Zheimer.'

Kilmore almost ruptured his neck with a triple take. 'But you should be off today,' he said.

'Oh no, old boy,' said Hardcastle. 'Today was yesterday. This is tomorrow.'

Kilmore noticed that Hardcastle had visibly grown younger and taller the moment he entered the theatre. This was his stage, and the Great Entertainer thrived on being on it.

'Ah, you have the patient all ready for me,' he said, expertly surveying the now prostrate figure of the Mayor, his stomach rising from the operating table like a large pink blancmange.

Both Kilmore and Tinkle were literally struck dumb as the master surgeon started to prod at the Mayor's enormous stomach with supple fingers that belied Hardcastle's age.

'Right,' said the surgeon, 'this is an emergency.

186

Scalpel, nurse. You, Doctor whatever-your-name is, you will have to be the anaesthetist.'

Kilmore, operating literally – and literally operating – on remote control, sent the Mayor into the land of nod with a prick of a needle in the arm.

As he was floating away, he could make out in the far distance a voice saying: 'I've got good news and bad news for you. The bad news is that I'm going to take something away from you. The good news is that by the time you come round I will have forgotten what it was.'

Suddenly Hardcastle was The Great Entertainer with a Scalpel in his Hand.

He pressed down firmly with his left gloved hand on the Mayor's lower abdomen and, with a quick downward stroke with the scalpel in his right hand, sliced a four-inch cut that brought the Mayor's rich red blood bubbling to the surface. There was a thump as Tinkle collapsed in a dead faint.

Kilmore wanted to say that the trouble had been caused by something that the Mayor had swallowed rather than any surgical problem, but his mouth was too full of fear for him to get a sound out.

Hardcastle made a second cut, this time criss-crossing the first incision. Now he had a flap of skin open under which he probed with his fingers. There was a second thud. This time Nurse May had fainted.

Gripping on to the side of the table to stop himself from joining the fallen, Kilmore at last managed to get some words out. 'I'm Dr Kilmore,' he said, 'and I need to tell you something.'

'Good show, old boy,' said Hardcastle, without a break in his concentration. 'I'm Al Zheimer.'

'This is the Mayor of our borough,' said Kilmore, 'and he has swallowed something.'

'I'm not surprised,' said Hardcastle, now moving lower down with his scalpel. This time he was cutting away at the Mayor's scrotum, and as he triumphantly removed Cocklewell's left testicle, Dr Kilmore took the fainting path to the floor.

It was several hours later when Kilmore, Tinkle and Nurse May were summoned to the private ward where the Mayor was recovering from his surgery. On the way they bumped into Matilda, who had just come out of the lift.

'You gave him the wrong tablet, you silly woman,' said Tinkle, still in a state of deep shock.

'What d'you mean the *wrong* tablet,' Matilda replied. 'I didn't give him any tablet.'

'What?' came the three-way response from Kilmore, Tinkle and Nurse May.

'I stupidly left the tablets at home in my flat and dashed home to fetch them during the tea break,' she explained. 'When I returned to the Town Hall everybody was in a terrible state and told me that the Mayor was dead.'

'Well he might as well be now,' said Kilmore. 'That madman Hardcastle has gone and cut one of his testicles off.'

'He's done what?' said Matilda.

'That's right,' said Nurse May. 'The Mayor's ball is

missing. There's been a right old palaver.'

'No, it's not right,' said Tinkle. 'It's his left one.'

They were all ushered into the ward where the Mayor was sitting up in bed with a man who looked like a lawyer in a chair alongside him.

'Ah, just the people I wanted to see,' said the Mayor. 'This here is my personal physician from 'arley Street, Dr Lionel Trimble-Smith. Costs me an arm and a leg, he does, but it gives me peace of mind to have him in my team. He 'as given me a thorough examination following my operation, and he tells me that I owe you people my life.'

There were suddenly four speechless bedside visitors.

The fifth was able to speak. 'But for your quick action in getting Mayor Cocklewell here to Haven Hospital,' explained Dr Lionel Trimble-Smith, 'he would have without doubt been beaten by what had become a sudden and rapid spread of cancer from his left testicle.'

Kilmore was first to find his voice. 'I think the vote of thanks should go to Harmon Hardcastle, the genius of a surgeon,' he said. 'But for him, we could never have saved the Mayor.'

'I did telephone the said gentlemen at his 'ome a few minutes ago,' said the Mayor. 'It took him some time to answer. Said summat about he thought it were t'front doorbell. I thanked him for all that he did for me, and he's invited me around for Malaysian tea with him and his wife, Agatha I believe he said 'er name was. Then he said something about being Algie Heimer, and hung up t' telephone.'

189

They were joined by the Matron and Clarence.

'Come here, you old battleship,' the Mayor said to the Matron, who was looking almost sheepish.

A shadow fell across the bed as the Matron pushed through to within reach of Cocklewell. He took her hands and kissed the backs of each of them.

'That's a kiss of make up,' he said. 'I'm sorry I caused you so much aggravation, and I want to say how impressed I were by your fighting attitude. I admire a lass with spirit.'

'Don't admire her too much, Mr Mayor,' said Clarence. 'She's spoken for.'

The Matron blushed. 'But what about the hospital, WC?' she asked.

'There's nothing wrong with our WC,' said Clarence, who was kicked in the ankle by the Matron.

The question the Matron had asked was the one that was bursting to come out of everybody at the bedside, apart no doubt from Trimble-Smith who could see one less loaded client calling on him at Harley Street.

'I've thought it through,' said Cocklewell. 'Look at this...'

He produced the local evening newspaper that carried the front page headline: MIRACLE AS HOSPITAL BRINGS MAYOR BACK FROM THE DEAD.

'Now I can hardly close down a hospital that has done that for me, can I. Haven stays open, and with an increased annual budget.'

Cheers rang out from the private ward, and down in the reception area Roper, Biddle, Shufflebottom, a drunken Clutterbuck, the almoner, the mortuary assistant – keeping a wary eye out for Dr Kilmore – and Mrs Wilton along with all the cleaning ladies hugged and danced with each other as they rightly interpreted the cheers as meaning the hospital had been saved.

'What about the supermarket?' Matilda asked.

'Oh that,' said the Mayor in a matter-of-fact manner, 'I'll 'ave t'police station knocked down instead.'

He was kissed on either cheek by Matilda. 'One thing, Tilly,' he said. 'Even though the Mayor's ball is off, it don't mean I won't still want dick-tation.'

'Oooh,' said Nurse May, 'I wouldn't mind 'aving a bit of that.' She let out a cackling laugh.

That was enough frivolity for the Matron. She clapped her hands. 'Come on, there's work to be done.'

She looked at Kilmore and almost smiled. 'Carry on, Doctor,' she said.

DON'T MISS THE OTHER HILARIOUS TITLES IN THIS **CARRY ON** SERIES

And don't forget that all the *Carry On* classics are also available on the Cinema Club video label, and distributed by VCI, price £4.99 each. Watch the videos, read the books... and *Carry On laughing*.